YEAR OF
THE THIEF

edited by matt digangi

Thieves Jargon Press *** Salem, MA

YEAR OF THE THIEF

Thieves Jargon Press
PO Box 2064
Salem, MA 01970
www.thievesjargon.com/press

Copyright © 2006
All rights reserved by respective authors.

ISBN: 0-9770750-1-X

Printed in the United Stated of America

First edition, first printing: May, 2006

All stories in this collection have previously appeared in the online literary journal Thieves Jargon (www.thievesjargon.com), except for Paul Kavanagh's *Gin*, Jeff T. Kane's *Help Me, I'm Hungry*, and Delphine Lecompte's *How I Quit Torturing Poodles*.

Cover illustration © 2006 Eric Jones

CONTENTS

THE THIEF

THE TODDLER SOMNAMBULISTS / 8
James Grinwis

SO OVER IT / 9
James Greco

EMERGENCY ROOM / 21
Andy Henion

HAPPY HOUR / 26
Mike Boyle

DISCO KILLED ELVIS / 30
Bradley Mason Hamlin

WHY THE DOG CROSSED THE ROAD / 32
Boz Bowles

ODEEN HIBBS / 36
Marvin Dorsey

THE MAGICIAN

THE ENTREPENEUR OF ROOM 303 / 40

Paul Silverman

THE CAGED BIRD SINGS / 49
Stephen D. Rogers

WHALEMEAT RETURNS TO SCHOOL LUNCH / 50
Corey Mesler

NEVER TELL YOUR BIRTHDAY WISH / 54
P.S. Ehrlich

WHISPER, CALIFORNIA / 61
Vishal Khanna

GIN / 75
Paul Kavanagh

THE FOOL

KERZ: MID-SEASON TRAINING / 92

Joe Shooman

THE IMMUTABLE LAWS OF PHYSICS / 100
Eric Jones

LIKE A THIEF IN THE NIGHT / 103
Malon Edwards

SCRAMBLING / 105
Tom Meek

SLUG LOVE / 107
Grant Perry

THE MOOSE HUNTER / 115
Dean Baker

WERNER SCHWAB / 120
Aryan Kaganof

HELP ME, I'M HUNGRY / 124
Jeff T. Kane

THE HANGED MAN

TAKE TWO / 134
Willie Smith

SNORT / 138
Daniel Allen Cox

A MAN IN BLUE / 142
Steve Finbow

SAMARITAN'S FLIGHT / 145
Suzanne Nielsen

3.8 SECONDS / 147
Matt Maxwell

IN DENA / 151
Ken Ryan

HOW I QUIT TORTURING POODLES / 155
Delphine Lecompte

CONTRIBUTORS' NOTES / 159

I

THE THIEF

THE TODDLER SOMNAMBULISTS

james grinwis

They are like rowboats half filled with brine. Yet they seem to bounce in the manner of androids, tiny bulbous heads with wisps of bedraggled hair, eyes overly rounded, little peg noses and mouths murmuring like the small trenches of running water found at the crests of tall mountains. Their fists are like dandelions and they sputter around, each one singing Sun, Sun, Mr. Golden Sun, please shine down on meeee...

SO OVER IT

james greco

Eugene has marvelous forearm hair. You stare at the warm curling brown thickness and figure it probably turns about golden on sunny days. You are captivated as he fries up some eggs. The hair down off his shoulders and out of his tank top is darker and coarser, but still remarkably nice for back hair. His moustache and temples are senescent; fifty to sixty-five depending on how reasonable life has been.

Pam needs new frames. She's early forties, jazzercise body, nice smile and great calves. She is sitting at the counter of the kitchen island, on a wooden stool with a leather seat, the paper folded to the crossword, waiting for the next two pieces of toast to pop up. And you wait for the next two pieces of toast to pop up too. There is a just discernable almost echo to the toaster that is unfurling, gaining pressure.

It wants you to slouch. It comes from your stomach and moves up through your neck and out of your mouth and pulls your face back down toward itself. You try to focus on sitting up straight and walking loosely, but it is there and it is tugging.

Pam looks up from her paper, needy. "How did you end up here with a job and no place to live…" she asks, reminding how you ended up in this scene: the room for rent. You sense Eugene's smirk from his shoulders and stare blankly. Your lips threaten to move. "It's usually the other way around," he adds.

"It just kind of happened. I'd been working at the bar for

a couple months and just got tired of going back and forth across the bridge. Then I saw the ad down on the community board and then I called."

Eugene turns from the stove with the pan in his left hand, the spatula in his right, preparing to slide the perfectly fried eggs onto one of the waiting plates already decorated with hash browns and toast. "How'd you end up at the bar?"

"Just did."

He does one of those shoulder shrug/dumb smile "Whaddaya gonna do with this guy?" things. You think of T-ball coaches, shop teachers, custodial engineers. The toast pops and you smile instead of shriek.

What would your idols think of this scene? Could they tell at first glimpse that this isn't lame, that this is just a quirky episode that probably won't even be discovered until your journals are published after your death?

The room is fine. It has clearly been revamped and is a little more modern in color, molding selection and furniture arrangement than the rest of the house. This is a furnished room, which is great because you can just go by the apartment when you know Cindy won't be home and grab the shit you need without worrying about any large items. You flicker onto Nonna's bureau, but decide to fuck it, things are stupid and do not preserve the people that gave them to you and *everything happens for a reason*.

She shows you around while Eugene heads down to the shop (he owns 3 bagel shops but is looking to sell them and get into PHO ["It's the new teriyaki"]). The house is big with much wood paneling and it is swelling in you how cool this all is. You're just like this post-fucking-hip guy that dropped out of the scene and got some weird room with a bizarre couple in the suburbs. But that's not even it, it's more like: This isn't rejecting cool, this is so much cooler than being in the band. This is like earthy and organic. This is how you learn, by mixing with real people.

Pam opens a trim closet in the upstairs hall that separates your room from the master suite, office and deck. She seems to expect some response and so you look. The closet is mostly neat, but the bottom shelf is cluttered and you let your eyes fall nostalgically over a hot water bottle and an old black head plunger and other items that have probably been in this closet since you were a kid looking over the same items in a similar closet in a home not far from this one.

"Well here's some towels and stuff you can use." Burnt orange or taupe, frayed at the edges, the towels seem to have been handed so many times— after hot-tubs or quick freshen up showers— to so many people.

"Thanks."

Pam does an odd knee-twist, self-aware body language thing. "We cook too much breakfast and dinner every day anyway, so…"

"Oh, great." You smile. It's true, this is all working out great. It will be like one of those sequences in romantic comedies where the guy shouldn't fit in but he does and then he does like all kinds of domestic stuff with the people he shouldn't fit in with and it seems more like family than a real family.

"But for lunch you are on your own," she says with sudden, false toughness. You think she could point with her finger and say mister sarcastically if she wanted to really drive this gag home.

"What's in here?" You point at a closed door near the closet.

"Oh, yeah," Pam dismisses and you decide not to pry. What if it's some room of a kid that died or like a collection of mummified dogs or something? It doesn't matter because this will be a good story and you are elated because you might sow with this woman and tell someone about it later.

It's weird always, when you think about it, how you end up where you are. At least, that's how you think about it. It's like this curious neo-bohemian, karma-enhanced, intrinsically linked series of events that has fated you into this ironic (or is it symbolic?) moment.

You are catching a break about 8:30. This is a good time because the dinner rush is over and the drinkers are just starting to roll in. You've got a burger and some mashed potatoes and Sharon snuck you a shot of Jaeger and your face is slick with the airborne grease and sweat from waiting tables. Your body feels utilized. You have an expanding magnanimity pulsing in your torso. You think you may have evidence that things are going to culminate. That everything is going to be—

"You feel okay?" Cathy asks. She's plump, but has a natural understanding of how to market her breasts.

"C-bone, I feel fucking stellar. Real top drawer…"

"You're a freak."

"Why?"

"In a good way." And she is gone.

And here you are in this place.

You're serving beer and you're working hard and only occasionally is a deeper opinion reminding you that you're living in a $400 a month room in some weird old couple's house because you are so fucking broke you cannot afford a single-person dwelling or consider your life outside of perilous 14 day periods. And it has been perilous. Though, based on the female reaction to your carefully self-effacing recount of your living situation, you were correct in the calculation that this decision was just offbeat enough to seem cool.

So, you are here right now and you are not in Austin or Detroit or Omaha or anywhere and that is cool because all of your idols used to be somewhere non-descript, surrounded by stupid people who didn't understand how special it was to be in their presence. And one day all of those people pause in their routines and see you on television and go, "Wow he used to…" and this is how your legend spreads and this is how you become important. You walk among them.

Eugene is making Monte Cristos when you get home. You've now, in less than two weeks, become accustomed to finding him cooking outdated sandwiches and improbable egg dishes in his boxer shorts late at night, but tonight he is in a nifty suit, with the tie undone and the shirt unbuttoned down low. Predictably, he has no undershirt.

"Count you in for a count?" Eugene says too quickly when you enter. Not like he'd been waiting to say it, but like it was a joke he has made many times.

"Sure."

He sprinkles some powdered sugar over the sandwiches and slides them onto a salad plate. They are quickly on the kitchen island and a bottle of Vermont Maple Syrup is produced.

"Hey look at this." He slides a clipped open magazine in front of you. Your eyes drift along an almost satiric ad for a household robot. But it is really genuine, from a name brand. You try to maintain eye contact with one of the kids in the magazine family and think about getting some robotic theme into your songs (if that hasn't already died).

"I gotta get back to the game…" He says contemplatively. "I leave half my money at home so I gotta come home and think about it before I spend it. Plus I get a sandwich." He delivers the last line as though it were a joke, but you can discern no joke and it is a little creepy the way he gives you that fatherly tug on the arm.

"Why did you show me this?" you ask, a little indignantly.

"I just think how funny we must seem trying to make our own robots."

And you decide if this guy is onto it, the whole robot thing must be played out. "Robots making robots?" you say, like a pre-teen hearing the same bogus historical fact his father always extols.

"Exactly." He folds whatever sandwich is left in half, gives it a squirt of syrup, and fills his mouth with it, hoisting his left leg up over the stool and turning to exit.

You finish what you want of the sandwich and leave the remains and plate on the counter. No one has said anything, but Pam is happy to clean up after you like she does Eugene.

You loll your way up the stairs. Coming up the last few steps after the landing, turning with the stairs you think you feel movement in the upper hall.

"Pam?" Nothing. You walk a few steps down, past your room. Their bedroom door is just ajar and you can see the ruffle of white duvet with ashen tint in the bedside lamp. She's not in there.

You move to the door. *The secret door*. And you stand and listen and maybe there is sound. Maybe you are hearing the reverb off something a million miles away. You trace a skull and crossbones on the door in the dark.

You think things are feeling frail.

So yeah, there are many reasons why things are good as you Cary Grant through the courtyard at Eugene and Pam's, blithely sidestepping a long forgotten big wheel, momentarily in a well-cut three piece suit, taking a 1940's drag of your

American Spirit.

For starters, you are done with work. Which is good because you are so totally over it and over all the discarded fries drowning in overzealous ketchup and embarrassing complaints about seven dollar steaks and bad jokes covering worse tips. And you are home. And home has become a picture in your mind and it is you in your room and on the bed.

You can visualize the pinched bowl in the cellophane from the tip of a cigarette pack stashed in your bedside table and a sudden rap-influenced feeling reminds you: Shit's been hella crazy lately dawg, you need to just smoke a bowl and chiiiiilll.

Secondly, that whole thing where you got to close up at 9 and everyone stayed and had shots and Kali got way too loaded and flipped you shit about the lack of phone calls post some recent alleged make out session and you got to program ALL the songs on the jukebox and danced with Kali to "Gin and Juice" and she dropped you off with another sick make out session, but no real play:

That was cool.

And now you're inside getting a drink of water and you're soooo ready for that bowl and like maybe some Conan. You are fixated on the humming of something (a troll?) under the refrigerator and swoon a little bit at the sink. There is a certain mechanical interference to your drunkenness. Connections are not being made. Metal is rubbing against metal.

A crazy ghost slaps you across the face or you have a mild stroke and then you are fine steadying yourself with hydration and thinking that if Kali would have just fucked you, you wouldn't be stuck here right now alone. And then you decide that sex is easy and patience is hard and that decisions we make to wait sometimes have more force than the decisions we make to act and Conan sucks but the weed is a fucking glass of milk after a work out.

You sit with your back against the wall and your shoulders cocked, you can feel your collar bones, like as their own entity, and your cheeks feel tight against your jaw and you've managed to keep your mouth shut for an extended period of time and there does not seem to be a crease on your angelic face.

You're thinking like, fuck, you gotta get a farm. Some place to grow your own food and like trade work for meat from local fowl and livestock farmers— or maybe hunters— or maybe just quit eating meat altogether— so you wouldn't have to eat any perishable or marketable food. How cool would that be? There is a knock on your bedroom door.

"Sam?"
"Yes?"
"It's Pam."

Pam, she, there's something silky about her. Maybe it's just the silk kimono-esque nightgown she's got on, but it's definitely something.

"What up Pam?"
"Oh, I, you know— Eugene isn't home yet."
"From poker?"
"No."
"Not even to get more cash?"
"No."
"Oh, I'm sure he's just winning— do you want to come in?" And she does and she wants to sit on the edge of your bed and talk and she wants you to be holding one of the two Bay Breezes she has with her.

And it is obvious immediately and you are so down. Because: How hot is this?

To fuck this older lady? Totally. There's all those like

MILF Hunter porno sites, and like Susan Sarandon or whatever.

It's totally hot.

"I'm not worried, it's only one."

"Those games go late." You're tired of hiding the pipe. "You want to smoke some grass?" It feels so sexy offering this old lady some weed. You gulp down the rest of your drink, but not like in a piggy way, like in a hole digging sexy guy way.

"Sure." And she takes it and smokes it expertly. She even does the little tap on the side of the pipe to loosen the weed up thing. "This is pretty tasty."

That's so cool, this lady saying that the pot is tasty. You see her at twenty, in sandals with spiky short hair laughing loud and talking shit to some meek guy who can't measure up and you remember that you are drunk and you note that you are experiencing some minor exchange of molecules that is generating a gravitational force that is drawing her closer.

"Do you have an erection?"

If you were on TV you would gulp.

"Yes."

"Isn't it weird how you can sit next to one person and get an erection or get wet and then sit next to someone else and not?"

"Yes." You can't help but agree that this is an odd phenomenon that deserves more study. You are clearly feeling buzzy or woozy, maybe boozy, maybe faint, or maybe elated. Maybe nauseous.

This is not the weed. Something is happening near your heart, there is a whole other caliber of disruption easing its way through your bloodstream. You wonder if people have E flashbacks.

"…and it doesn't matter who they are or where they are from. It can be anyone. And people always meet someone and think how amazing it is that they have met someone similar to they are and it's fate that out of all of the people in the world they have found someone like them without thinking, that – *HEY!*– if someone is similar to you, has a similar past, it stands to reason that their present will be similar too. It's not a miracle that the folks you met are similar, they're just on the same grid." You are looking at this woman and she is Janis Joplin, or maybe Joan Baez, whichever is the hot one. Something is slow, this is on 77 speed.

"Unless you make a point of randomly meeting people, you'll never know who really floats your boat." And then she goes for your cock.

"Yes," you stutter in agreement with this whole premise. The whole line of logic that results in Pam putting your dick in her mouth is a good one and to be agreed with. And you have all of the evidence you need. There is no doubt that cool is something someone innately is, that the world comes to you. You float with the tide and follow tracks in the dirt and sniff out the truth in the wind and you are led to situations that are indicative of how you are and what you deserve. All you have to do is say yes.

"Let's go in the other room?"
"Yes."

The other room, *the secret room*, is blurrily weird and seemingly not the former, or current, lair of a dead person or animal.

It's all chiffon. Is that a thing? Chiffon? Maybe.

It seems like a platform in the middle of a plush pumpkin with fuzzy corners. This room is not round. As she lays you back on something that is like a doctor's table there is an externally motivated, video produced reminiscence to the motion. You feel truly fortunate.

She grinds onto you and you can feel all of the edges of your face and decide that everyone can fuck off. You're sick of it. You go into the city to bars and to the record stores and everyone has their own little scene and they protect it so hard and devote themselves to knowing and redefining constantly what is cool so the herd can be thinned and they can feel special. Like you go to buy the new Liars CD and you can't just buy the Liars CD, you have to buy another CD too because you don't want the condescending counter guy to like think you're eagerly waiting and waiting to get the new Liars CD or, worse, that you are just hearing about the Liars for the first time, responding robotically to some carefully low key, multi-tiered publicity and advertising campaign.

And as you feel your abs tighten with slick penetration, you are gaining momentum and you're just like: fuck everybody and their whole categorization and qualification of who and what is cool. You know things in your blood that could send these worthless hypocrites determining the validity of your actions running in shame with their mesh trucker hats on fire. And the rest of the world would know and understand and, presumably, dance in the void of their dissipated treachery - and what the fuck is that one lady doing with your wrists? Putting them in straps?

Funny straps?

That would be so fucking funny if she was like hooking you into some sex chair. No, no, better yet: she drugged you and is locking you into some sort of sex machine. And you grin at the thought of a weird dark secret and see yourself confiding it later and like how your eyes seem.

This is the you that braces, back to the wall, just around the corner, waiting for just the right moment. This is the true end of the prequel, the beginning of the ascent. You are standing on high, the sun is on your back. This is a coronation of the you that will conquer and show mercy.

Some darkness catches a view of your vainglory.

That sequence starts where they play back all of the scenes from the movie that add up to the big reveal and you see everything clearly, reversing course. The coolest people in the world aren't cool. And not like in the 80's movie not knowing you are cool is cool kind of way. Like: They are also operating solely in opposition to mental visualizations of what other people must think.

You know super-suddenly that your most self-possessed idols wake up in the middle of the night gasping for air, convinced marauders will bust through the door at any second, exposing them as fakes. There is nothing cool inside them, they do what they do and are deemed cool by people that have something to sell.

This all builds in a symphonic crescendo with an eaten cassette tape warble. That nagging squirm at your center is not just hang-ups, it's not as simple as fear. It's something important telling you—

You become unexpectedly aware of Eugene in the room and recognize that this has some abstract relationship to the topic at hand. You see the error in your process and know you have figured this all out too late. As you feel his stubby carpenter's finger smear some KY Jelly over your anus you know: *This is it!*

EMERGENCY ROOM

andy henion

I inform the clerk through a vent in the glass that a pack of thugs invaded my home, drugged me with an unknown substance, cut off my right pinky toe and left me to bleed out and perish. The clerk clutches her sweater tighter around her shoulders and without making eye contact asks me a series of questions including health history, insurance information, blood type, employment status and next of kin, inputting all this data into a computer with two bored index fingers. The process takes upwards of twenty minutes and at one point I remind her that a digit has indeed been extracted and she says, We'll see you as soon as we're able, sir, and later on I explain that I am lightheaded and close to vomiting and/or fainting and she motions to the bathroom at my immediate left and adds that if I do in fact disrupt the registration I will have to go to the back of the line. Just as we're completing the process, two ambulances arrive delivering what I take to be high priority cases judging by the frantic actions of several nurses and doctors who descend on the gurneys and begin shouting familiar medical jargon and conducting drastic procedures such as mouth to mouth and cardiopulmonary resuscitation. A man sitting in the waiting room wearing a grungy Cheerios baseball cap and missing at least two front teeth grunts audibly and complains to his two female companions that now it will be another three goddamn hours before he is seen. One of the companions must be his mother because she also is in dire need of dental work and tells him in a maternal tone to Shut the fuck up, Billy Joe, this ain't no fun fer any of us.

I limp painfully to one of the few vacant seats in the waiting room and along the way detect an assortment of unpleasant scents including malodorous footwear and glandular discharge. Across from my seat is a teenage girl surrounded by two toddlers with greenish snot dried under their noses and on their cheeks and chins. All three of the youngsters are dead still and staring straight ahead as if they are genetically predisposed to behave or perhaps severely sick and lethargic or perhaps on some type of adolescent control medication. The teenage girl is stick thin and wearing a flannel shirt, a miniskirt and purple cowboy boots. She is slouched down in her seat with her legs spread and I have to work to keep my gaze from falling on her matching purple panties. The stick thin girl stares at me without blinking for so long that I look away to the sliding doors as if I am waiting for someone to arrive and when I look back she says, Where's the toe? and I say, The toe? and she says, I heard your story up there, so where's the toe? I say, I suppose the thugs kept it for a souvenir, and the stick thin girl says, What did they cut it off with? and I say, in a low tone, My, ah, tin snips, and I fully expect the stick thin girl to laugh aloud at this fact but instead she just nods as if this is what she had expected.

At this point an adult male and female come through the sliding doors and walk over to the three youngsters and the adult female says, Get your shit ready and let's go, and the two toddlers climb down off their seats and retrieve tattered bookbags and stand straight up and down as if at attention. The stick thin girls tells the woman that she is going to hang around for a while and the woman looks at me and then glares at the stick thin girl for a few moments before saying, Close your legs, you little whore, and then the whole family minus the stick thin girl proceeds to make its way out of the emergency room in a single file line led by the adult female. When they are gone the stick thin girl says to me, The kids come here to warm up after school while the two of them are out doing their thing, and I think, Doing their thing? and I say, Don't you go to school as well? and she smiles for the first time since we began conversing and says, I'm nineteen, guy, and this surprises me greatly based on her pubertal facial structure and diminutive stature.

The stick thin girl tells me her name is Paul, which is short for Paula, and asks me where I am going. I am not sure what she means by this, exactly, so I say, Hopefully back to get my toe stitched up before I expire, and Paul says, No, after that, and I say, Who said I'm going anywhere? and Paul says, We're all going somewhere, guy. I think about this for a moment and say, Well, I have decided to drive down and see my wife and son in Dubuque, and she says, Now we're getting somewhere, Big Daddy. But there's no way in hell you're driving halfway across the country in your condition. You'll need a companion, and it just so happens that I'm heading that way myself. At this point the man with the missing teeth and the Cheerios cap comes steaming up the aisle ostensibly to deliver a complaint to the registration clerk and as he passes my location his heavy work boot slams into my bloody toe hole which is covered only by some gauze and an athletic sock and I scream and feel the nerves of my foot explode up into my groin and the Cheerios man stops and laughs at my predicament and I have a very strong urge to stand up and knock out even more of his teeth but the urge to pass out is marginally stronger…

There's a physician standing above my feet with a British accent and sunshine yellow hair, although in truth that might be the effect of the surgery lights.

There's another physician punching the British fellow in the upper arm playfully and teasing him about his recent date with a nurse from the sixth floor whom he proceeds to call a German shorthair, which in turn yields a round of laughter from the entire surgery staff.

There's a nurse with a wide face and continuous eyebrow referring to me as Darlin' and stroking my lower abdomen to provide comfort. There may be an erection at this point.

The physicians are now debating how the loss of a pinky toe affects walking, swing dancing and other forms of human movement.

There's an orderly mopping the floor and possibly rifling through the pockets of my slacks, which have been folded neatly and placed on a counter next to a hard plastic container of bandages, syringes and various other medical supplies.

There's the stick thin girl manipulating my genitals in a furious fashion as I drive eighty miles per hour on the interstate toward Dubuque. This clearly is not part of the surgical process but instead some type of dream, perhaps triggered by the nurses' rubbing of my lower abdomen and/or the pain medication that has been injected into my vein. There may be ejaculation at this point.

There's a police officer at my bedside with a cocked eyebrow asking me to explain these alleged suspects who entered my home without invitation. Alleged? I say, and I believe I may be slurring. Nothing alleged, all confirmed. And the officer says, Sir, the doctors tell me you had massive amounts of street narcotics in your system. Can you imagine this in the newspaper tomorrow? You really want to push the home invasion angle on this thing? Incredible, I say, or at least I try. You think I cut off my own toe? Sir, I also understand your wife left you recently? Took your young son along? That's enough to drive a man to the extreme right there. Jesus Christ, I say, or at least I try, and I close my eyes and shake my head and try to forget the police officer and his ludicrous queries and instead occupy my mind with my pending trip to Dubuque and a travel companion named Paul and the dried, hardened patch that's pulling the short-hairs of my lower abdomen.

HAPPY HOUR
mike boyle

She told me her name a few minutes before but I had forgot it. "I try to keep 100 poems in the mail," she said.
"100?"
"Yes."
What can you say? That's nice? Do they all come back?
"So, you're a poet?"
She downed the rest of her shot and took a swig of beer.
"Yeah, man. Like you," she said.
"What?"
"I know you, Jack. Fucker." She gave me that look. She knew me. In on a little secret. Had the big picture. "Why don't you come to the readings anymore, Jack? You too good for us?"
"Look. What's your name again?"
She told me and then went to the ladies room. I forgot it again. Another 10 hour day in the factory. For some reason, I thought of her as Jane from the Fun with Dick and Jane books. See Spot run. Run Spot, run. There was a cat. Puff?
I looked over at this guy a few stools down. He was sneaking sniffs of something he took out of his pocket. Took a big huff, shoved it back in his pocket and looked up, over at me. His eyes rolled back in his head and then his head hit the bar. It was happy hour.
Jane came back as Brenda, the bartender, was trying to wake the guy up. Brenda patted his head. "Hello? HEY!" His head rolled a bit like a cueball afterthought but he didn't fall out of his seat.
"He might vomit," I told the Jane girl.
"Ewww."

"Is he dead?" I asked Brenda.

"You wanna help me with this guy, Jack?" Brenda asked.

I stood up and went over, felt for a pulse on his neck. "Still alive," I told her.

"Could you please get him out of here?" she asked.

I yelled over to Billy, who was talking to some woman on the other side of the horseshoe bar. We dragged the guy outside and sat him on the sidewalk, up against the building just as he was coming to.

"I'm gonna kick your ass!" he yelled.

Billy laughed and I told him I'd be back out in a few minutes.

Back inside with the girl I thought of as Jane. Brenda gave me a beer. "My hero," she said. Hours drinking. Talking nonsense about writing. Her 100 poems in the mail and my 10 or so. Her readings and writer friends. My tirade about the folks at poetry readings.

"Look at this!" I showed her my knuckles that had been skinned open earlier that day.

"Ha! That's nothing! Look at this!" She lifted up her shirt and showed me her appendectomy scar.

I went to the pool table and she followed. I didn't care. I ran the table and busted a few sharks out of the bar. They were humiliated to be beaten by an obvious drunk. They had brought their own sticks and I had used the bent bar cue. I put my arm around her waist and laughed at them as they left. Then, nobody wanted to play me anymore.

"C'mon, Jack," Jane said.

"You're all a bunch of weaklings!" I yelled out at the bar.

Eyebrows raised, Brenda gave me the look. I swilled down the last of my beer and went over to the bar, set it down. "Brenda, I love you."

"Get out, Jack. Come back tomorrow," she said.
"C'mon, Jane. Let's get out of here."
"Paula. My name is Paula."
"Right."

We went outside. The guy that wanted to kick my ass was gone. She was saying things. I took her by the hands and kissed her, slowly started to spin around. Started spinning faster, we were at arms length and I spun and laughed, looked up at the sky. Streetlights, stars. Van Gogh chopped off an ear and mailed it to his brother. I wanted to get her feet off the ground.

"Jack! Let go! I'm getting dizzy."

"I'm gonna fling you into the trash cans so you can be a real poet!" I told her. My knuckles started bleeding again. "Ahaha!" But I knew I couldn't do it. I was a failure at writing, at commerce and at gymnastics. I stopped, let go. We stood there for a bit.

"Aren't you dizzy?" she asked.

"I have a huge aerobic capacity," I told her.

"You got blood on my hands."

"Sorry."

I wiped my knuckles on my jeans. Cars were wizzing by on 2nd Street. I gave them the finger. Nobody honked or yelled.

"You're a good kisser for a crazy person," she told me. "I live over there," she pointed.

"Over there?"

"Yeah, by the river."

She told me the name of the place. Swank digs. Lawyers, disc jockeys and girls with 100 poems in the mail.

"Look," I told her, "I'm going to meet some people. Walk with me a bit, OK?"

I took her arm and walked north. Tomorrow would be the

factory again, condescending looks and general mayhem. There was a flower bed; I ripped up some flowers and gave them to her, roots and all.

"Oh, Jack."

She smiled and shook off the dirt. We kissed again. My one knuckle was still bleeding, dripdrip. We got to the corner.

"Always remember this," I told her.

"Well, where are you going?" she asked.

I looked up the block. There was a gang of blacks and bikers hanging outside John's Place. I saw someone whip a bottle and then another. There was some yelling. Somebody was probably holding. Nobody would ever paint them or write about them.

"Up there." I told her. "You coming?"

"No freakin way, Jack," she said.

"Yeah, well, it's probably better. I'll walk you home."

"You don't have to do that."

I told her to stop and walked her home. The guy that wanted to kick my ass was at John's but he wasn't saying much. My old junkie friends were there. Jane had given me her number and I felt it in my pocket.

DISCO KILLED ELVIS

bradley mason hamlin

In 1977, in Los Angeles, we watched TV.
Lots of it. All of the shows good in that bad mainstream funky disposable way.

Love Boat and Fantasy Island.
Happy Days.
Chico and the Man.
Phyllis. (Copout: My mom watched that one.)
The Sonny and Cher Show.
And others…

So there I was: sitting on the black leather couch in our living room, a good place to let the world spin. You could spill beer (if you could steal beer), wipe it up, and no one would know.

I was watching TV.

I had just smoked one of my mother's Salem cigarettes in the bathroom and felt a slight head rush. Half a joint and a green apple later — I felt okay. Life was simple. The Fonz snapped his fingers and said, *"Heyyyyyyyy!"*

I liked that.
Crazy.
Stupid.
Simple.
Shit.

Suddenly a fat guy in a white Vegas Liberace clown costume leapt onto the screen. The sweat of pills and girls and liquor and too much love leaked out of his face and dripped down his sideburns.

Fucking beautiful.

"We interrupt this program to bring you the tragic news on the

death of an American legend. At… blah, blah, blah… today… blah, blah, blah…

"Elvis Presley is dead."

My mother walked in from the kitchen, drink in hand. Her face looked almost as tired as Presley's. She slurred something. Then she slurred something with the word fuck in it.

"Mom?"

"Yesh?"

"Do you think it was the drinking?"

"What, Elphis?" she asked.

"Yeah, you think all the booze and stuff killed him or do you think it was like… a government conspiracy?"

"Nooo. Drinking never kilt," she hiccupped, "anybody. Just bad feelings, just bad situations. Bad luck."

In 1977 I was fond of the Ramones and the Sex Pistols. Radio was dying under the disco lights and the approaching corporate takeover.

"Disco?" I offered.

"Huh?"

"Disco killed Elvis."

She thought about it.

"Maybe," she said. "But nooo," she finished her drink, "I think … it was just all the people."

WHY THE DOG CROSSED THE ROAD

boz bowles

Doggie wasn't quite dead yet, not after crossing the heavily pot-holed stretch of asphalt twisting through loblolly pines like a sludge mired stream. Salty smell of squirrel piss on the breeze, juicy luscious squirrel; it did, in fact, taste like chicken. Or enough like chicken, to dogs at least, to make his saliva flow. But it didn't smell like chicken a bit. Fur always smelled better than feathers, which clung longer in his shit, waving in the breeze like teeny fans, temporarily keeping away flies.

No need to jump for chickens. They don't fly really. But squirrels, once they're up a tree, that's it, they're gone. On the ground, Doggie could run them down, step on their backs and rip them open with his teeth, sending them flying and flopping back to Earth. Squirrels' death spasms always seemed like a taunt to him, all herky-jerky, suddenly slower, then silently still.

Doggie, whose name was Poopie—an unfortunate name, yes, damage done by a long-missed child who knew no better, who often chased Poopie with a chewed wooden baseball bat—had remembered to look both ways, but the blacktop was cold and its hardness hurt Poopie's toenails, so he crossed the road slowly, looking down at his puffs of breath against the yellow stripes on the gray road. Poopie recognized the sound he heard, his own panting, was somehow connected with his breathing. Poopie realized, at that moment, he was breathing. He thought about it as much as his doggy little brain could, and he thought *breathing*. His thought surprised him. Not his idea of breathing though. He was surprised by his own act of thinking. He had never known of his ability to think before. Until now, all he ever thought was *squirrel* or *chicken* or *poop* or *human* or *warmth* or *cold*. Or *bitches in heat*. And he hadn't really been aware of his thinking even at those times. But now he thought about thinking. He thought about having a thought, his thought.

Balls, he thought, and it was satisfying to think it, so he sat right in the middle of the road, curled down over his belly, and began sniffing, then licking his cock and balls until hair started sticking to his tongue. He snuffled, stopped for a moment to look around, giving the air a quick sniff. Squirrel piss, a touch of his own shit stuck in the hair around his tail, and a little taste of his own piss, his calling card for all the local bitches. He returned to licking his sack sloppily until his old familiar red-tipped friend poked through the wet curl of hair around his shaft. He licked the lipstick head of his little doggy dick right there in the middle of the street as flashing images of stinky bitches, fatty hunks of meat, cool rainwater, and all the other sensual comforts of his life ran through his mind. He thought about human affection, the rubbing of his belly, flopping of his ears. He thought about the joy of watching local cats run under porches and up trees, their bellies low to the ground as though they thought they might be flung from the world if they stood too tall as they ran.

Then he thought something new: *car*. He smelled the heat of the tires first, friction against the cool asphalt that by now had become comfortable under his tail. Then he saw the red and black thing coming around the bend in the road, tiny in the distance, but coming, growing, like it had been hiding behind the trees, waiting for him to be distracted.

I've got to move, he thought, but before he decided whether to dodge left or right, he hung his mind up on the first part of his thought – *I*. This was the same *I* that breathed. This *I*, this thing that enjoyed dew, ate chickens, shat feathered turds, licked its own balls, fucked all kinds of bitches in heat. This was the same *I* that breathed steamy puffs of breath. This *I* thought. He enjoyed his thought of *I* so much that he began to say it. He began to say "I." At first it sounded like a cough, short bursts of air again showing themselves as steam, hanging in the background of road and sky. He tried again, and this time he did it. He said "I" in a voice so loud and clear that it blocked every other sense from his mind. He reveled in the sound, feeling the vibration of the word in his entire body, but especially in the pleasure centers of his belly, his balls, his ass, and his mouth. The word echoed through his head, vibrating moist warmth through his mind like that of his momma dog's belly just before he was born into this cold, honestly lonely world.

He was so stunned by the sound of his own voice that he forgot the growing sound of the engine, the crescendo of tires against pavement, whining with their own kind of petrochemical pain. He was so taken aback by this sound of "I" that he ignored the big red and black blur of car, getting bigger as it came, louder, rushing up, pissed off and just cocky a bit like all cars seemed to be. He barely noticed when it lifted him up off the ground by shoving a corner of fender through his liver. Two strands of small intestine were ripped out of Poopie's gut and pulled down the highway. Poopie got dragged along with them.

Poopie lay on the edge of the road and saw his stomach ripped open. It didn't hurt him a bit. He felt lighter, like he could roll over backwards without any effort at all. He didn't have a belly to worry with any more, but his own stool was strewn all over hell. He didn't have to chase any more squirrels or chickens or wild turkeys or chipmunks forever. He could stretch out on the cool asphalt road and think about how light he felt for the rest of his life. And just what did he mean by the rest of his life?

While he lay there bleeding and dying, neither perturbed nor unperturbed, and realizing for the first time ever that either option could actually happen to him, two other cars ran over his bowels, stretching his eel-slick and pinkish intestine further into the road. One car was a gray '92 Ford Escort, the other a big green Peterbilt dump truck. The bloody slush of Poopie's guts against the asphalt smelled akin to a sack of vomit dropped from a school bus window.

As Poopie bled to death in the road, his blood rolling into the pool that extended the line of his shadow into the grotesque, yet interesting and even familiar shape of a cave drawing animal, he thought about the warm bloody salt of a fat young squirrel in the fall. He died with a playful breath, blowing imaginary chicken feathers off his blood soaked tongue, fearless in violence and not a notion of himself in death.

ODEEN HIBBS

marvin dorsey

The spring air breathes through the leaves of the oak tree in the back yard. He drifts back and forth, suspended in the porch swing, hung from the limbs. His old bicycle leans against the side of the workshop, an artifact from his past.

He notices, as he gazes into the lit windows from the back yard, that the boys and his daughter are engaged in an animated conversation, probably about the NCAA playoffs or James, a neighbor kid, who, in a fit of bravado last week, climbed on top of his father's pick-up truck and touched the power line with his tennis racquet. They were passing on their way to soccer practice. "Look, it's not killing me!" his silly grin proclaimed. And it didn't.

He's amused and comforted by his children's excitement and the rare occasion when they are not bickering with one another. Ty, a skinny thirteen with crew-cut blond hair reenacts a flying slam-dunk, while Coleman, eleven, an experienced raconteur himself, patiently waits his turn to tell of an even more rad phenomenon. Simone, nine, sits wide-eyed, not quite believing the tall tales.

He's forty years old, wears Air Pegasus running shoes and owns a construction company. This morning he scanned the classified ads for a used Porche 911 he plans to buy and fix up, ostensibly for the kids, when they reach driving age.

An airliner silently crosses the night sky on its flight path from Dallas to San Antonio. The red beacon pulses like a tiny heartbeat in the gulf of darkness sprinkled with stars. As if gravity were suspended, it scribes a perfect arc across the darkness.

A wave of fatigue overcomes him as he contemplates this

now seemingly strange and futile vocation of resisting such a constant and pervasive force. He orchestrates a cacophony of laborers, craftsmen, and subcontractors. They build foundations, then columns and beams, roofs and suspended ceilings, all in an effort to hold out against gravity. He remembers what gravity did to Odeen Hibbs. He remembers that moment, on a windy day, when Odeen, handling a large sheet of metal roof decking, was blown off the roof of the new Cotton Exchange building. Odeen, clutching the sheeting, attempting to catch the air with it and sail down to safety. Curiously, for that first moment, those watching thought he might do it. Sail that sheet metal down to the ground from six stories.

That instant of irrational and collective hope that Odeen could manipulate that floppy sheet of metal into some sort of kite or hang-glider confounded him now. The moment quickly passed. They all shared Odeen's terror as the sheet metal buckled like a broken wing and he fell, never closing his eyes.

He looks back at the airliner, receding into the distance. He wishes now that the airliner was Odeen Hibbs with the sheet metal, the red beacon being his heart...bleep, bleep, bleep...sailing across the sky.

II

THE MAGICIAN

THE ENTREPENEUER OF ROOM 303

paul silverman

Haggerty was a Catholic patriarch, the old school. So when he found out Francine, his art-photographer daughter, had been seen leaving Room 303 at the crack of dawn, his face got as purple as a bishop's cloak and he pinched his praying, sniveling wife. Haggerty's style was to pinch instead of punch. Little merciless pinches all over Dottie's spare tire and thigh rolls and bat wings. He would hold a pinch for thirty seconds and twist it. But this the world never saw. Assumption College loved Haggerty's ass for the student refectory he built, in a style the school's consulting architect dubbed "medieval industrial park."

It so happened Francine had the functional tits that were Jitzy's favorite kind. They were thin and pendulous – nothing like the ones in the magazines, except National Geographic – and maybe they weren't for everyone. To each his own. But when Francine was in Room 303 straddling Jitzy and they were swinging down around his head they looked about two feet long, like the party balloons you can squeeze and bend into animal shapes.

Theirs was a match made in black and white with a matte finish. Francine was of the Diane Arbus school – *a freak to you is all of humanity to me*. In her field of vision Jitzy was a subject sent down from Hasselblad Heaven.

And Haggerty was all wrong about his daughter and Jitzy anyway. Francine wasn't doing one-night stands in the Holiday Inn. It's not a one-night stand if a woman of forty-four is visiting a man of forty-two in his home.

Why, it was Haggerty himself who had started calling Jitzy

"the man who lives in the Holiday Inn." Just to taunt him like a helpless dog – because he thought it sounded funny – because it made Jitzy into one of the lame ducks of life, as Dottie once put it. Secretly Dottie *liked* to think of Jitzy as a charity case. Every time she sent a casserole over to Room 303 it made her feel higher in the food chain. It was her form of pinching.

And then the workers and fellow salesmen picked it up and they always said it too - in a snide way – *Look, the man who lives in the Holiday Inn* – as if they all dwelled in really, truly better places. With their split levels and their sump pumps. Well, as Jitzy's mother used to say, they could all go shit in their hats and pull it over their ears.

It just made sense – given where he was, given what he was doing. He was staying in Holiday Inns all over Hell's Half Acre anyway; crisscrossing the land from one to another. He was getting used to the way they did things. He liked the security of not being able to pick up a table lamp because it was bolted down to the nightstand. If you couldn't pick it up you couldn't knock it over, and if you went bananas or something, or someone else went bananas on you, nobody could grab the table lamp and crash it against a wall or break your skull with it. When you're starting to think about living on some piss-poor pension and social security and Haggerty's handouts these things become important to you.

Better to make some deal with a nice Holiday Inn in your local area now and move in and be done with it. Jitzy could count, he could add and subtract. He could see the cruel path of inflation written on the wall – on the happy Holiday Inn wallpaper – and he wasn't about to wait until it dropped him down the chute to Motel Six or Econo-Lodge or worse.

His furnishing needs were minimal. A closet pole and hangers, and a bed that was hardly king-sized. He had smoked since he was nine years old and maybe this had stunted his growth. He still bought his clothing items in the boys' department. But being a shrimp had advantages non-shrimps can't even imagine. It made Francine's breasts seem even longer, like the drooping ears of a giant rabbit. When she loomed over him on all fours he pillow-talked her about tying them around his head.

Do your ears hang low?
Do they wobble to and fro?
Can you tie them in a knot,
Can you tie them in a bow?
Can you throw them over your shoulder
Like a Continental soldier,
Do your ears hang low?

For a shrimp, Jitzy could carry one whale of a bag, because he was born for it. In younger days, when he was a bellhop at the Ritz, the elevator broke down and he carried a bag that was bigger than he was up eleven floors. He carried it for an old man with a stained tweed suit who wanted him to stay and play for his tip. Jitzy did what he had to do and got out of there. Why is it the whole world thinks aging bachelors who move into the Ritz to live out their lives are privileged and elegant? But a man who lives in the Holiday Inn is daft and dangerous, a pervert who might prey on kids at the pool? When Jitzy finally quit being a Ritz bellhop you could drive a truck up his ass and there would be passing lanes on the sides. In the Holiday Inn you carry your own bags and stay out of trouble. It's the American way.

If Holiday Inns are anything, they're convenient. Jitzy's was equi-distant from the Springfield and Hartford airports and a stone's throw from the Dispoz-a-flame headquarters, warehouse and showroom. Room 303 was not too high and not too low. It gave its permanent occupant a sweeping view of the Oldfield strip mall and the dirty gray hills beyond.

The strip mall was a bonus. The Holiday Inn was so contiguous it felt like a limb jointed to the K-mart. On cold days Jitzy could walk from his room to the K-mart to the food court without spending more than six seconds outdoors. Francine would send him down for props – Halloween masks – while she set up the tripod.

Be that as it may, Jitzy still picked Haggerty's cotton. He lugged the big Dispoz-a-flame and Dispoz-a-flash cases from Skowhegan to San Bernardino, humping to make quota and beyond. Only Haggerty himself was a better salesman, because he was so evil.

"Those Frenchies can make pens," he'd say to customers, dissing the Dispoz-a-flame's rival lighter, the Bic. "But trust them with lighter fluid, never. Remember the War."

Jitzy never changed a sheet and he never cleaned the toilet. He had new neighbors every night, on both sides and up and down. He always had fresh mini-packs of shampoo by the tub. He stubbed out his cigarettes in ashtrays he didn't own, and the maid dumped the ashes and butts. He never unpacked his suitcase. He traveled four days out of every seven, carrying Dispoz-a-flame lighters and Dispoz-a-flash flashlights to smoke shops across the land. Wherever he went, they put him in Room 303, so he was home and away from home at the very same time. That was the marvel of the Holiday Inn. Let Dottie Haggerty prattle and cross herself about family dinners and tree houses and peewee hockey and her thirty grandchildren bobbing for apples in front of the hearth. Let Haggerty throw another log on the fire and pound his chest about owning the prettiest piece of God's country east or west of the Yangtze, where Red slaves fabricated the Dispoz-a-flame gold-toned caps.

No one has a deed on God's country, he told Francine.

"Twist your body," she said, aiming the Leica. "*Contraposto*. Now put on the space helmet and think of landing on a distant star. Do not smile."

All Jitzy had to do was pick up the phone for a wakeup call. Long as he lived he would not have to purchase toilet paper.

Haggerty wanted you to think he, King Haggerty, owned everything. He owned a racehorse at Saratoga. He owned Francine until the church might join her hand in marriage - and he swore such a union would not be, not while he drew breath, to a cretin half her size.

One day Haggerty called Jitzy into his Normandy Tudor office and held an eight by ten glossy of the horse under Jitzy's nose. "Can you find the nuts?" he asked.

"Not on him," said Jitzy.

"Fair warning," said Haggerty, flicking a custom true-gold Dispoz-a-flame under the tip of his Cohiba.

But Francine still spent that night in Room 303. And Jitzy dreamt of the starry desert, his tent a canopy of teats. But only for so long.

For this was a night to remember. The night of the Big Boom.

The ear-splitting force of it nearly broke the Richter Scale at the Assumption College lab. Next came the marshals, the ATF and the regular cops, who did enough interviews to make a case file taller than Jitzy. They dug into everything and everyone. And why not? The conflagration, after all, was the biggest ever in regional history. A pre-dawn blast that lit up the countryside, rocked the dirty gray hills and even made the Holiday Inn buckle.

During the dead of night the Dispoz-a-flame warehouse had burst like a nuclear bomb. A half million gold-toned lighters exploded sky-high. Barrels of fluid ignited and launched the roof like a NASA space station. Everything blew to smithereens and there was nothing left, not even the bronze miniature of the racehorse Haggerty kept next to the Archbishop's autographed picture.

Jitzy's phone rang at 4 a.m., some time after the thunder-sound. He tumbled out from under the fleshy arbor that was Francine and drove to the disaster site, now a hosed-down, smoldering heap. The cops threw yellow tape around the whole perimeter and seized everyone inside it as arson suspects. As the first rays of sun peeked over the dirty gray hills, Jitzy had to sit captive while a raincoated shrew with big ATF letters on her back jabbed at him with trick questions:

"So when you got out of your car and approached the building, how tall were the flames?"

"What flames? I didn't see any flames."

The fire police grilled him three times. Ditto Francine. Ditto Dottie. They went after anyone and everyone whom Haggerty had usuriously screwed. But in the end, like all cops, they targeted the candidate most vulnerable to a case they could actually win, guilt or innocence aside. And this was Haggerty himself.

The motive the D.A. cited in court was the kind that always sways juries of common citizens. A whopper of an insurance policy whose sole beneficiary was Haggerty. So fat was the award he actually doubled his net worth the moment the last lighter blew towards Jupiter.

Haggerty pulled every string in his vest pocket, but even the Archbishop's secret visit to the judge's chambers could not stem the onslaught of pyro-experts brought to the witness stand by the blood-sniffing D.A.

"I personally found accelerant traces at various points in the rubble," testified a state college prof, the very one who taught the six-week arson crash course that gave the fire marshal his credentials for office.

"Jesus Christ knows I make cigarette lighters!" screamed

Haggerty, terrifying the jury. "*Accelerants are my business!*"

In the end the gavel banged and Haggerty drew a ten. All his uptown lawyers could do for him was win Corrections Department assurance that he'd do his time in a facility where he'd be safe from assaults on his property and his bum.

So the feudal baron Haggerty, like the peon Jitzy, went off to spend his sunset years living in a room he didn't own – a room so many notches down from Motel Six and Econo-Lodge it made the Holiday Inn seem like The Four Seasons. Like Jitzy, he never had to buy toilet paper.

And all he could do with his Normandy Tudor mansion was continue making the payments, using the sum from the insurance settlement, which a civil judge reduced considerably after the arson conviction.

One day well into year three of the sentence, Jitzy came to see him in an entrepreneurial flush. He proudly pulled out a smashing sales report and traced the columns with a pencil, giving Haggerty the history as he went along. Ever since the lighter business went to hell the night of the blaze, Jitzy had quietly thrown his energy into the second and weaker product line, Dispoz-a-flash flashlights – whose warehouse and inventory sat in another town, uncooked and clean as a whistle.

Watching the firemen comb through the black wreckage with their long heavy lamps had given Jitzy an idea. He began calling on municipalities, positioning his compact, featherweight disposable flashlights as a space-age ergonomic tool enhancing firefighter agility. At first no one listened. But inevitably…

"Detroit wants twenty thousand," he exclaimed across the table to Haggerty, pushing the spreadsheet under the prisoner's mortuary eyes. "We can roll this out everywhere."

But all Haggerty rolled out was a cello-pack with his daily

meds, the generic uppers and downers dispensed by the state. He swallowed three tabs and sat like a stone statue, cold as one of the lions that flanked his former driveway, until the guard said time was up. In captivity, all the fire and brimstone was gone.

Even wearing his highest elevator shoes, Jitzy was a peanut compared to the burly penitentiary officers. He trotted past the last of them and then ran into one more, at the dirt lot beyond the ancient brick and shiny razor wire where they had made him leave his car. He was patted down and finally allowed to set forth on the long ride home, a solo journey that gave him three good hours to reflect on Haggerty's complete implosion behind bars.

The man was a yellow bag of bones, as burned out as his storehouse of Dispoz-a-flames. He was Haggerty mourning Haggerty.

More than ever, Jitzy saw it was immaterial whether Haggerty had ever lit the match. His crime wasn't arson; it was ownership: the belief in his own divine right to possess whatever he touched: people, places, chunks of the earth – as if the whole round world – the oceans and seas and trees and warehouses and slaughterhouses and even the Big House – weren't what they were: all one fucking Holiday Inn where everybody was just a guest with a checkout time.

Jitzy drove under the happy green sign and found his favorite space, right under the tier of balconies. The year was rolling around to the season of cheer, and the air was crisp as a red apple. He went up three flights in the elevator and unlocked the door to Room 303. A present was waiting for him on the freshly made bed – Francine on all fours, her hair long and silvery as tinsel. He ripped off his suit from the boys' department and slid under her, watching the hair cascade around his face, a forest of tinsel just for him. Then he moved down and found her breasts, dangling before his eyes like Christmas bells. Flat on his back he inched forward – until they just bumped the sides of his face.

What she said to him was out of a dream. And maybe it was a dream.

"My father was a big man. I want a little man."

When he raised his head a bit he could see between her legs to the wall, where his sturdy Dispoz-a-flash case stood filled with flashlight samples in engine red and safety yellow, everything ready to go. On top of the case was his plane ticket.

Tomorrow, the Chicago Fire Department. Chicago, Chicago, Chicago.

THE CAGED BIRD SINGS

stephen d. rogers

The view from up here is incredible and makes me feel as if – I don't know – as if I can begin all over again.

There's the valley down below, the rolling hills, the highway crossing the bridge that spans the mighty river. It's all so far from where I started that it seems possible for me to become a completely different person.

Why not jettison the past? Why not create a new me, a new future, a new life? "Today I am rehabilitated."

My arms aching, I let go of the bars and land on my feet.

My cellmate snickers.

WHALEMEAT RETURNS TO SCHOOL LUNCH

corey mesler

Whalemeat strode in like a highwayman, let the doors swing free behind him. It had been months, several months, following an ignominious departure, an expulsion complete with constabulary. Several repercussions followed his exodus from Hugo Ball High School, sometimes called High Ball. Lately, Whalemeat had been brooding about the school's gym teacher, Mr. Drawcansir. Coach D. His sandy crew cut, his bigotry, his exquisite harrying. Whalemeat felt the time was right for a return. A squaring.

Again: Whalemeat strode in like a highwayman. He spotted Bandy Lyle Most first thing — good old Bandy, with his crooked head and expressive mouth. And Whalemeat's old sweetheart Lila Palooza, still wearing her tits on her chest, still smirking to make boys wilt in the heat. Ah, Lila, if there were more time.

Whalemeat swaggered into the great unwashed gaggle, eyes red as a wasp's sting. Once here he was king. The remaining rat pack knew his name. They whispered, "Whalemeat, when he was here it was the teachers who learned." Or, "Whalemeat, come to me tonight when the helmsman's bark of old ferries to hell the dead." Textbooks corrected themselves. Thesauri roamed the halls, feral and antagonistic.

Whalemeat smiled at Lila, remembering her revved up in the Hurston's treehouse, her rubbery body a recreation. Lila, she remembered, too. Her smirk died on the way to Whalemeat's heart. She reached out for him, once, her hand a wobbly shoofly. Whalemeat simply parted the freshmen, their faces red with propinquity.

Coach D. recognized Whalemeat. His face palled, his lunchmeat turned viridian. To be confronted on his home turf, and during School Lunch! It was grotesque!

"Drawcansir," Whalemeat spoke in a whisper. (Later, it was said that his dropping *Mr.*, or *Coach*, or some said it was his voice, as quiet as dreaming trees, that spread a frisson through the cafeteria like an electric charge. It was said that all students who had not yet reached puberty reached it collectively at that moment.)

Drawcansir never even puffed up. He never had a chance to affect the tough. Where was his usual pugnacity, his vicious tyranny? Gone like a shape in a vision. Poof.

"Uff," he managed.

Whalemeat began his sinuous move toward him. The Students at School Lunch were immobile as if gorgonized. Lila took the nearest freshman boy's hand and placed it inside her bra. The freshman petrified.

"April 16, 1973," Whalemeat said with the calm of an executioner.

"Is?" the coach sibilated.

"The day, the day you thumped my friend Bandy on the head. Thumped him like one would an insect. And said, with your customary eloquence, 'You're a pussy'."

Bandy's head bobbled. *"This is for me?"* he said to himself.

Whalemeat turned toward his friend. Yes, he thought back. Yes.

Coach Drawcansir was contemplating this boy-man, this Whalemeat, who had expanded during his absence. He was a gorilla, for Godsake. A Goddam gorilla. He seemed as big as bull-beef, and tough, as if weathered, as if hardened by the devil's nagnails. And those eyes—

"I didn't kick you out, friend," Coach said, his voice unexpectedly there, oiled with a trickster's wiliness. He suddenly believed he could slither out of this sticky wicket.

"Ah, Coach," Whalemeat said. There was that whisper again. "This isn't about Whalemeat." Whalemeat squinted at Drawcansir, his concentration a sniper's. Some say it was a dream, a group-sleep. Coach Drawcansir was unexpectedly withering, shriveling, and contracting as if made of residue. He dwindled like a spent pizzle.

It was Whalemeat's glare!

"What, what?" Drawcansir squeezed out, his voice diminuendo.

It was those eyes!

"Heey," Coach peeped. "Heeeelp meeee."

Those eyes—like a diamond's cut blaze!

Whalemeat just stood there, a Colossus, and watched as his former adversary telescoped downward. The student body aged years—they were spellbound. Their coach, their very own Fuehrer, was teensy, a piddling, pint-size pygmy. A fog fell over the assembled, stunning them into silent reverence.

Then, as sudden as a thunder clap, they hoorayed as one.
Hooray!

Whalemeat! they cried. Whalemeat the Vindicator! they shouted. Whalemeat our Paladin!

Bandy Lyle Most walked over to the shrunken former persecutor and picked him up under the arms the way one might a stray cat. He looked him straight in the peepers. Coach Drawcansir's eyes were pitiable, brimming with a lifetime's tears. Bandy set him down, ran a hand over his crewcut tiny head like a Chia Pet. He then bent over and whispered, "Go away, little man."

And Coach D. did. He beat a fleet retreat.

Some say he ran until his little legs about gave out. Some say he ended up several states away, in a small town called

Banana Oil, whose population never left 3 digits. Here he stayed, a small fish in a small pond. And he never bullied another soul, not even a dog, a stoat, or a skink.

Whalemeat became the foosball coach at Hugo Ball High. Foosball.

The first year his boys went 12 and 1.

The next year they were undefeated, won state, and their crack player, Sam Onides, skipped college and went straight to the Pros, made millions, married Lila Palooza, etc.

Whalemeat, well, he is a legend around here.

Although, some say that day at School Lunch never happened. Where there is magic there will be scoffers. We all live in terminological inexactitude. Whalemeat understands this. He doesn't take the doubters personally.

NEVER TELL YOUR BIRTHDAY WISH

p.s. ehrlich

As we're seated she whispers that if by any chance I have a present to give her, I mustn't do it here. "Then they'd know it's my birthday and bring out a cupcake with all the waiters singing and make me blow out the candle in front of everybody. I would just *die*."

Her couple of drinks translate into six frozen daiquiris, half of them peach and half banana. Her food she barely touches. The result at first is kittenish, then increasingly antsy. Hectic little laugh. Twittering jitters. With a fidgety flourish she pulls off her wedding and engagement rings and throws them into her purse.

"Today I am no longer Mrs. Marco Formi. As of right this very minute, I'm single Judi Dahl again. Oh thank you—" to the waiter, serving daiquiri number five.

"I'll still call you Dee," I say.

"You better! Dee-e-e-ar. And never 'Joo-girl,' no not ever." Gulp of rummy banana purée. "I always declare inpeden – inpeh? – inde*pen*dence, on my birthday. Took off my scoliosis brace on my sweet seventeenth... and then that booger Chad I was going with who got off on the brace went and *dumped* me."

"He must've been an imbecile."

"Well I showed him. Three other guys asked me out right away."

"Good for them. Your filet's getting cold –"

"And then on my twenty-fourth, I did it again. Bigtime. Gave up giving him second chances."

"Who? Marco?"

Another gulp. Finger crooked at our waiter. "Just one more, please?... Yes – Marco. If I so much as *glanced* at another man, even only a passer-by, he'd yell like I was cheating on him. And I NEVER did. But the things he said... and did to me... finally I couldn't take it anymore. We were going out for dinner, I didn't want to but it was my birthday and what he says goes, see, so right there in the car I blurt that I'm leaving him. He just throws his head back and laughs. Then he says... he tells me... if I do, if I leave him, I'm going to end up as a, a, a—"

"Dee—"

Spitting it out: *"A crippled old hunchback."*

Her stark white face goes to pieces. She ups and turns, fumbling blindly for her purse—I hand it to her—get a garbled *Thank you*—before she runs off to the Ladies.

Other diners eye me. So does the waiter, from whom I accept daiquiri number six. Which I'm too designated to drink, badly though it's needed. I stare back at each eye, and each is averted.

Judith reappears, walking very straight and tall. Face reassembled, makeup reapplied. I stand, half-embrace her, hold her chair; she sits.

"I'm so sorry."

"No, no."

"I shouldn't have said anything—"

"No, no—"

"—to *him*. Not before I blew out the candles. Never tell your birthday wish."

"Well..."

"He was driving. When he said that to me. And broke my heart. And then we crashed. And he got killed. But I was thrown clear. Just some scrapes and bruises. They were worried about my spine, of course. Couldn't believe it when they couldn't find anything wrong with it—anything *new*, anyway. The doctor said it was a miracle."

I take her ringless hand. Seems like the right thing to do. She presses mine and says something I can't quite hear.

"What?"

"...then he came back."

"When—?"

"A year later. A year ago. On my twenty-fifth. It was a really bad day and I went to bed early and lay there grinding my teeth. And I saw him. He came back and showed himself to me."

Shrill giggle: brittle harpstrings.

"How—?"

"I wasn't dreaming!—not at the time. But I've been dreaming about it ever since. Him. It. And now tonight..."

Better get her the hell out of here. Too much to handle otherwise, especially if she finishes that sixth daiquiri.

Outside, thunder is rumbling. Whole damn world sounds Wagnerian. And Judith wants to get behind the wheel. "I can drive. Give me the key. It's my car!"

Lightning flashes, she gasps and jumps; I bundle her into the shotgun seat. Now to Sycamore Terrace, as fast as possible. Let her just sulk quietly all the way...

"I'm not some dumb jockette, you know! I was an education major! I got my teaching certificate! *Je peux parler Français!* AND it's my birthday!!" She grabs hold of my right arm, digs into it with her nails, then starts sliding that hand up—

—and it is two years ago and I am Marco and I have broken this lady's heart at its most vulnerable point, so that she unbuckles her seatbelt to guarantee oblivion before reaching over and yanking the wheel, I am Marco feeling the car leave my control to veer and smash and throw Judith free, seeing this with my last sight before the final impact—

—and it is now and I am me and traffic is light, coming and going, so I chance a direct look into her angry midnight blues and say, "DEE!—"

She looks perplexed. "What?"

"It's just me here, dear."

"I know that," she says. Sliding that hand back down to my elbow and squeezing it.

Hottest night of the year and I am all ice. After getting her safely home I should borrow this car, drive myself home alone, bring it back tomorrow. "Er, Dee—"

She looks away. "I'll do anything you like if you'll stay with me tonight. All night. With me. And not on the sofa this time."

Icebreaker.

We make it to Sycamore Terrace. I park the car below its cunning little canopy.

"So will you? Please?"

I look at her. "Till you tell me to leave."

She looks at me. "I love you so very much."

"...You better have this, then."

She perks up, opens her birthday present. "Ohhhh... Put it on me?" She extends her left wrist; I add my silver bracelet to the bangles already there. "Yes," she says. "Oh, yes."

Oh, yeedge. There speaks a woman. I get out, go over, help her out and up and along, she frankly hanging onto me.

"I knew it was you the whole time," she murmurs.

"Well, don't let that bother you."

She strums her harp and lets us into her place as the first drops of rain start to fall.

Inside, so much black hair is floating around I think her cat must have blown itself up. Suicide backfire, perhaps, or spontaneous combustion? A hope that's dashed when Noir's head pops out from beneath the sofa, making us both gasp and jump.

Judith bends precariously down to coo at the head, which looks terrified. Another rumble of thunder: the ears flatten, the maw opens, and the head retreats out of sight.

"My kitty doesn't love me anymore!" wails Judith. "But *you* do, don't you? Let's see how much—"

My only concern about stripping in her living room is that her beast might leave its lair to deposit mementos in my shoes.

"Smile for me, honey."

I strain instead. My *schweinhund* is now a purebred foxhound.

"And you've got a—?"

"Right here, yes ma'am." Roll it on and we're ready to rock.

Her boudoir: my first admission thereto. Narrow cot beside the window. Air redolent of girly potions, fabric softener, Lemon Pledge. Dominating the room is an antique rosewood armoire, solid and vast. Any other time I might scrutinize it with a woodworker's eye, but Judith has shut the door behind us and started trying to wrestle her dress up over her head.

The armoire can wait.

I get the dress off her and wonder what to do with it— drape it over something? Stick it on a hanger? But now Judith is tipsily twirling as she removes layer upon layer of undergarments. My old-fashioned girl: many a slip 'twixt the skirt and hip. Dancing a connubial ballet, piling my arms with her white linen and nylon and lace. And inside my head I hear: *Am I beautiful?*

Too mild a word.

What am I, then?

You are transcendent.

Smile for me, so you'll be too.

I do. Despite my foxhound's relentless Lookit those! Lookit them! Lookit that!, I feel oddly at ease, as though this has always been our nightly ritual. She is not a sculpture or a robot, but graceful young intoxicated femininity. And what's sauce for the goose—

Can I be on top? My spine, you know.

Anything you like. Just have mercy.

Outside the rain falls harder.

Double-snap of leghole elastic—

And a CRACKLEPOP shakes the room, flickering the lamp. Judith leaps and gets her toes caught, trips over her panties and falls onto the bed, rolling onto her back, arms and legs spread wide—

She can be on top later.

Drop her duds and mount my charge—

"Oh," she goes.

"My," she adds.

THUD

THUD

THUD on the door—

"NO!!" she yells in my ear, "HE'S HERE!!"

—thrusting me away from her, altogether out and off and up to stagger back against the door, my hand instinctively finding and twisting its knob—

"—DOOOOOOON'T!!—"

—as in flies a dark blur landing between her splayed legs lunging up her front like a sex-starved ghoul intent on incubusing as it drives her clear up the wall pinning her there knocking an Our Lady off its shrine empurpling her face as she expels every ounce of breath

from her powerful swimmer's lungs in a godawful scream completely drowned out by the

B-W-A-A-A-M-M-M

of a transformer exploding nearby and killing all the lights—

Blackness.

I stumble and blunder and spill, trying to find her, to hold onto the sound of her gibbering *HolyMaryMotherofGodprayforussinnersnowandatthehourofourdeath*, but there's a roaring noise rising in my ears and—

—curtains, their cord, wrench it off-balance, and I see no more than I could before.

"Dee? Judi? Judith?"

"GET OUT OF HERE!"

Not near the bed. More like from within the wardrobe. Hiding inside, behind her clothes? Search for a latch—

"GO AWAY! I HATE YOU!"

Sounding further away. And then, as if from some abysmal distance:

"LEAVE ME *ALOOOONE*—"

So I do. Though I can't be sure she's talking to me.

WHISPER, CALIFORNIA

vishal khanna

Boys are delicate and can break in the wind. They fall to pieces. The rain makes everything sick. Dangling at the edge of the cliff. Water a crash. A bloodbath. A clock stops and minutes become days.

The highway winds toward the scattered lights of the city. I swing a moss-covered stick in my hand and knock it against rocks on the side of the road. The rocks make a hollow sound, like a lobotomy patient.

There is a torso of a squirrel, haloed by a ring of blood, on the side of the road. I tap it gently, turn it over. The belly is rotting. Slits of skin exposing food for worms. Satanists live in the mountains and the mentally disturbed need less oxygen to survive. Water supports life and is strongest when it floats below the clouds. The smell is overpowering, a pocket of death, but I do not look away. What is inside the hollowness is what I am searching for. My name is Violet Wonderland and everything is a shade of gray. My boyfriend is dead, trapped within the confinement of a dying Cadillac, and I have nowhere to go.

A car stops ahead of me and parks in the dirt-covered shoulder. The passenger door cracks open.

The driver's name is Freda. She is in her mid-thirties and her belly is huge. She may be stuck beneath the steering wheel.

Do you know Lamaze, she asks me.

Breathe in, breathe out, I say.

Freda's hair is bleached white. She scratches her head, her brick red skull. I think it's a load of shit, she says. I'm gonna get filled with drugs. I do not want to be there, whenever it happens.

She shifts gears. Her arms are so frail. Her body does not match her belly. Her stomach looks painted on.

You ever think about having kids, she says.

I don't answer.

If you want to smoke, go ahead. I don't mind.

I light a cigarette and reach to roll down the window but I stop. I see my reflection in the glass. A smear of reds and purples across my face and the smell of death in the air.

It's electric, Freda says. She rolls the window down. Air rushes in and it feels like there are holes in my head.

Where are you going to stay tonight, she asks.

Don't know, I say. I'll figure it out.

Why don't you stay with me. I could use the company.

I don't want to impose. No. What about your husband.

No husband, no man. Just me and the little one. She pats her belly. Stay at my place, she says. I'll make you dinner.

Freda's house is an A frame in the University district. Broken beer bottles in her yard and the sound of grasshoppers and car screeches coming from the street. Freda looks at me, she rubs her belly.

This child. The husband's probably putting his kids to bed. I can see him, kissing their foreheads, smiling, exposing his shark teeth.

He's married, I ask.

Full package. Wife, three kids, house in New Irving Park.

She pauses, looks around her living room. An aquarium, a black leather couch, a white vinyl massage table.

I've been running all my life. I get too close to a man and the bell rings. It says, Run Freda. Get away before it's too late.

I get on the massage table and lie on my side. The tension inside a blanket that surrounds me.

Why don't you take off your clothes, she says.

What.

Take off your clothes. Freda slides the back of her hand softly against my torso. I'll give you a rubdown.

It's her house and so I slide out of my dress. No bra and I am lying on my stomach in my panties and Freda slides her hands across my body.

You're so tense. What have you been through, what have you seen.

A moon setting in the mountains. A cloud rising above and fading away.

Freda moves slow, her belly is weighing her down, but her touch is smooth and gracious. I close my eyes and see flashing red lights. I open my eyes and see that the sun has set. A fade to sleep caressed by the hands of this woman whose skin smells of lavender, this woman who may or may not be a dream.

It's time, it's time.

It's four in the morning and Freda is screaming. I quickly get dressed and run to the bedroom. She is lying in bed, a helpless look plastered across her face.

My water broke, she says. Her pajamas are soaked and she is curled above the covers.

I'll take you to the hospital, I say. We'll get you drugs.

I help her dress and grab her small suitcase from her closet. She slides into the backseat of the car. I drive to the emergency room. Lavender comes off her skin like a blast of aerosol. Her face soaked with sweat. My heart beating so fast but somehow I slip into composure and get her checked in.

I pace around the waiting room for half an hour, watching the broken faces of the southern middle class. Two women, one in her sixties and the other half her age, crouch around a worn bible and recite in whispers.

A man, tall and dressed in a maroon three-piece suit, sips from a cola. His free hand holds nervously to a courtesy phone and I wonder if there is anyone on the other side of the line.

I have no idea what I am doing here. Two days ago, I was in the passenger seat of Moon's car heading west for San Francisco. We were planning our lives together and leaving trails of cigarette butts across the interstate. And now I am the sister lover of Freda who is having a baby five hundred feet away from me. I am homeless in the town I grew up in where I have no family and no one I would call a friend.

The man in the maroon suit is holding the phone at his waist. There are tears coming from his eyes. I walk over to him.

Can I have your cola, I say.

He hands the drink to me.

I reach my arms around him and hug him and whisper in his ear, It will be alright.

And then I walk out of the hospital. This is really none of my business.

A five-gallon jar filled with ashes. Eight a.m. and the sun is no weapon against the crisp winds. I block the wind with cupped hands and light a cigarette. The moon has set, I know this is true, but I stare at the sky hoping for one more glimpse of its whiteness. Just one more glimpse is all I want.

Scars on my left arm from sleeping on concrete. I pick at them below the sleeves of my jacket. I close my eyes and feel the bones that ache from the city and think of the cushioned seats of the Cadillac.

A man in a blue suit walks by and I ask him for change but he doesn't even look at me. I know things need to change soon. The weather is getting colder. Compassion is a fluid and freezes in the winter. I am a cold blooded animal and the chilly air flows through me like an IV unit.

At the shelter eyes are knives and callused hands take whatever they please. I bite an apple and suck its juice. I am curled in a corner and stare at my fingernails. Billy Squier is playing on the radio. Stroke me, stroke me.

This place is removed, cold and impersonal. The black and white tiled floor covered in dents the size of fists. Fading paperback books on a wooden bookshelf. Stacks of paper napkins everywhere. Three men sit at a table and play cards. The deck is made of notebook paper and covered in fingerprints.

There is an old woman dressed in a blue sweater with holes at the elbows. She stands facing a wall, holds a piece of green chalk in her hand and draws a picture of a three-legged horse.

I walk to her. I want to touch her, caress her and bring her back. A hand across the back of her hair and she turns to me.

The blood is yours.

What, I ask. What are you talking about.

The blood, it's yours. On the cuffs of his sleeves. It's yours.

I am about to ask her what she means but the shadow of

a man cuts me off.

Violet, he says. His hair is long and natted and he smells like cheap detergent.

Ralph.

When d'you get back, he asks.

A couple of days.

You hiding from me. You been back two days. Jesus, Violet. Where the fuck's Moon.

Still going west, I say. I hand him the half eaten apple and turn back to the woman, but she is gone.

Where'd she go, I ask Ralph.

Who. What are you talking about.

The picture of the horse is gone, replaced with a mirror hanging on two bent nails. The image of Ralph. He looks younger, his hair is straight, short like it used to be. This is not the right image. I turn around and his hair is long again.

Ralph, how you been. I lightly touch his cheek. It's rough, it feels scarred.

Don't touch me, he says. You don't know. You had to leave with him, didn't you.

I was in love with him, Ralph.

I was in love with you.

I'm sorry, I say, it's not my fault.

I walk past Ralph and toward the door.

You fucking broke my heart, Violet. You tore me to pieces.

The door closes behind me and Ralph becomes a silence and the silence becomes a soft purr of traffic, this velvet clamor of a city's mechanical noises.

A sun hiding behind ink filled clouds. The air is thick with humidity and tastes of rain and pollution. I exit the street through a black painted door below a graffitied sign.

The back table of the Gentleman Serf. I ash my cigarette

on the tiled and spotless floor. The walls of the club are round and smooth. This place feels like an oval mansion. Framed H.R. Giger paintings hang evenly on the maroon painted walls. Twisted cyborgs with alien faces. The few neon signs are hidden near bathrooms and exits. A woman in a tight green tank top stands behind the bar. She dumps a bucket filled with ice in a sink and I hear the sound of steel against steel.

A man, bald and in his forties, sits down across from me. He takes a drag on a cigarette. His lips are puffy, like he has had collagen implants. A slight breeze circulates through the club, disseminating the smell of imitation cologne, of Johnny Walker Scotch. His bare head as oval as the club.

You don't have any problems, do you. Tell me now young girl and we won't have to worry about it later. There's still time to go back. To where you come from.

No problems, I say. I can do this.

Why don't you take your clothes off, he says. Let me see what you got.

You first.

He takes a long drag on his cigarette then says, Fair enough. He takes his shirt off. His chest is shaved and completely covered by a tattoo of a raven. The bird only has one eye. It stares at my chest.

Caaw, caaw, he says. Your turn.

I stand up and pull my dress off. My nipples are cold, they harden in the view of the raven. I walk a few feet to the side but the bird's eye does not look away from me.

How do I look, I ask.

How do you look. Gorgeous, he says. Purely gorgeous, my sweet.

He points to the bar and says, Talk to Rain. She'll tell you everything you need to know. You'll start tonight.

Rain is a young girl. She doesn't look older than fifteen but

I am sure she is at least twenty. She has short bleached blond hair that looks like a helmet on her head, a silver lip ring crusted with blood. Cream colored skin and the tank top she wears barely covers her breasts.

She sees me look at her cleavage and says, Bartenders don't make as much money in a strip club. The bills all go to the dancers. We got to battle with something.

She pours water into a glass, mimicking the way she would pour a shot for a customer. She leans over and shakes her chest and gives me a smile that I read as fake but know drunken men would read as foreplay.

Nice technique, I say.

You learn quick that you have to do whatever you can that works. I'll show you the dressing room.

I follow her past the bar and below a neon sign that says Employees Only. The dressing room is small, maybe twice the size of the stage. There is a coffee maker and a small fridge in one corner and a row of elementary school desks against a wall. A long mirror drapes behind the desks and scattered lipsticks and glosses are on the tabletops.

There are two posters on the opposite wall. One is of a woman completely covered in metal riding a flesh colored motorcycle. The other is a safe sex promotion, a cartoon of a hot dog wrapped in plastic.

Rain escorts me to a desk at the far end of the room. Your desk, madam, she says.

Alone. Dressing room. Staring at the mirror. Don't recognize face. Skin is wrinkled and covered in thin cuts. Pink, watered down blood. The glass shatters. Turn the desk around and face the Metal Woman. A long spiral scar across her forehead and cheek. She smiles at me. I smile back, politely.

Three fifteen-minute dances and one hundred dollars in tips later. I am standing outside the back entrance of the Gentleman Serf. My head is killing me. Each glare at my body tore away some secret part of me. I counted the beads of sweat on their faces. Twenty-three per dance. My skin was so cold. I couldn't focus on their eyes. I looked at foreheads, drops of sweat like marital tears, the cuffs of their sleeves like dead skin on snakes. And I danced within that dark covering of aura thick like dried toothpaste.

The exit of the club is nondescript, a worker's entrance. Rain walks behind me and lightly touches the back of my neck. Removed and strangely sensual, a feather dropped from a tree. We walk to her apartment where I will sleep on the floor. A place to fade out of this hammer against my head.

Her apartment is tight and small, like an alleyway. A bed in one corner, a black beanbag chair in another, a tiny hallway that poses as a kitchen. Nothing else.

Will the beanbag be alright, she asks.

Anything is fine.

I curl up on the floor, using the chair as a pillow and fade away to the rhythmic beating of my temples.

It is morning. The sun shines angrily through Rain's window. There is a body behind me. She is naked, curled into the curve of my back. Her hand holds mine across my chest. I squeeze her hand then turn over and face her. Wrap my arms around her and she feels like a child within my wings.

I'm sorry, she says. I was lonely.

She rests her head on my neck. This is a sexual feeling but it is also the feeling two lonely people have here at the edge of this cliff. It is morning. The naked girl in my arms is beautiful and warm and I want nothing but to hold her forever.

It's alright, I say. It's fine. Go back to sleep.

There is a dove within my grasp. A frail and smooth dove that in some secret world thinks I may be her mother.

Goosebumps across my belly. The scent of musk in the air. Rain is pulling off my panties. My shirt is on the floor next to me.

Rain, I say.

Don't worry, I won't. Just let me do this.

She drops my panties next to my feet and I say, Okay, okay.

Her cheek pushed against my breast, the warm touch of her breath against my nipples and I don't know how to describe this. She moves up and kisses me on the neck and then she kisses me on the lips and I kiss her back and she says, I won't, I won't. Her feet slide across mine and I feel her push against me. She is wet and smooth and gentle and her tongue is the healer of souls. Her breath is cool and soft and her lips trace down my body until she is between my legs and I say, over and over again, Okay, okay, as I let her heal me.

Moon is driving. I search for a tape on the dashboard. He turns to me. It's really coming down, he says. Yes, I say, it is. I put the tape in. It's Billy Squier. I rest my head in Moon's lap. Whisper California. The rain, he says, it's really coming down. Yes, I say. Rain is the healer.

Rain makes us a pot of coffee. She gives me a dress to wear. It is tight on me, she is half my size, but it is better than my dress that has weeks of wear trapped in its folds.

Rain is sweet, she acts like a child. Her voice is high and

she skips around the room. She says it is because I have made her happy.

Is it because of what we did, I ask.

No, Rain says. I did that because you needed it. I could tell, you know, you needed someone to touch you. But that's not why I'm happy. I'm happy because of you. I haven't had a friend in so long.

Rain is from a small town in the mountains of Tennessee. She tells me that her father disappeared when she was eight. She has a picture of her mother on the windowsill. The woman looks old, at least sixty, and it surprises me to hear that she is only forty-seven.

Where is she now, I ask.

Still at home. She's a paramedic at the hospital in Knoxville. She met a man a few years ago. Bud. He's a truck driver. He's never around though. She gets lonely, calls me up and cries. I tell her to come down here but she won't. She says it's her home up there.

These streets are lonely. I have a friend who says she will heal me but the bright sun is still darker than the night. The faces of strangers flash in x-ray vision, walking skulls. I am a worker bee, I think. I have no idea where I am anymore. I think this is the town I grew up in, but nothing seems familiar. The buildings are odd, they look warped. I see my reflection in the dark glass the first floor of a Woolworth's. It's a funhouse. I'm eight feet tall. Plastic Woman. I smell lavender in the air.

A man bumps into me and I fall to the ground.

I'm sorry, he says. Are you all right.

He gives me his hand and pulls me up and I see it is Ralph.

Hi. Ralph. I'm all right. I'm fine.

Ralph wipes the dirt from my dress then says, I talked to Moon earlier. He's in town.

What, what do you mean. He's in town. He's here.

Yes. I just talked to him. He said he was looking for you. He wanted me to find you. Bring you to him.

Ralph, where is he. Take me to him.

I walk through the city streets behind Ralph, blindly following him. My heart is racing, I can't believe Moon is here.

He takes me to the Gentleman Serf.

He's here, I ask. What's he doing here.

Moon's inside. Heard you worked here. He came looking for you.

Inside the club, three people are sitting around a table. It's Raven and Rain and Freda.

What's going on here, I ask. What are you all doing here.

Raven stands up and faces me. Sit down, Violet. Please, sit down.

Okay, I say and sit next to Freda.

Raven is above the table, circling, pacing around. He takes his shirt off and stops.

Wings of raven move. Flap flap across the man's skin. Pulling at his flesh haphazardly. The eye closes. It opens and looks away. It looks west.

We are in the Cadillac, heading west on Interstate 40. The floorboards covered in fast food wrappers and empty packs of cigarettes. There are two billboard signs on the side of the road; one advertising a strip club, the other a smaller sign that says, Knoxville, 23 miles. The rain attacks the windshield. Shadows of mountains are monsters watching our progress. Moon looks at me and smiles.

It's really coming down, he says.

I lean my head in his lap and close my eyes. I can feel his warmth.

Yes, I whisper, it is.

Moon's lap is a resting place, a safe haven from the rain and the past.

Moon.

What, Violet.

What do you think about the name Freda for our baby.

I think I am dreaming. A stage. A dark room. Men in suits stare at me. I am wearing a g-string and dance around a pole. Smoke rises. Mauve shadows surround me. This round and smooth room. Rain pours ice cubes in a sink and there is a storm. The moon has set. I'm crying, I think. Wet drops across my face. Everything is wet. Puddles of black water. I am crying, I know I am crying. A car hanging off the road. The front end smashed in. Smoke, it fills the interior. A mess of something inside. Misshapen, strange. A billboard sign above the car, the lights dangling dangerously above. Smoke rises in a mauve haze. I am on the side of the road and don't know how I got here. A raven above circles me and watches. It watches me and watches the car.

A man stands above me, the cuffs of his sleeves covered in blood. This blood, it must be mine. What happened to you, I ask. He says something, I see his mouth move, but I can't hear him. A siren in the background. Red lights flashing everywhere. The smoke, it rises. It reaches through the rain like a shapeshifter.

It's time, he says. It's time. The ambulance is here. A shape in the smoke. Hazy lines. Leaning into each other. A three-legged horse.

The horse runs away from here. It never looks back. It sees where it has to go and disappears before we have time to say goodbye.

GIN

paul kavanagh

Fate. That word. Fate. An intruder enters a home in the early hours. It is still dark. He finds himself before three sisters. He points his gun at the head of the middle sister. He is unaware of the sharp bread knife between his thighs. He knows he has to kill all three sisters. He looks at them dressed in their white sheets already like ghosts. His finger feels the trigger but before he can pull his arm suddenly becomes numb. He looks and sees the youngest sister with a hammer. The gun falls to the floor, his broken arm to his side. The sharp bread knife slices through his jeans and other materials and lacerates his penis and genitals. Prostrate upon the hard wood he hears the oldest sister pull the trigger. Is the story about the Greek word *ate*? And what about *Moira*? Homer speaks of a single moira, a mysterious power to which even the gods are subjects and whose decisions were irrevocable. *Moirai*, those vixens! Thebaid used the appellation: The Elysian Sisters. Was it the intruder's lot? I'm leaping with alacrity ahead of myself; I will only get vertiginous and lost if I continue at this pace. The story. We have to blame any unaccountable personal tragedy on their lot, their portion. In the corporeal, in the temporal we have to say that the Gods had a hand in the tragedy. Monotheism, polytheism, it's all the same when we need to lay blame for a catastrophe. And so the birth of *Moira*! Those goddesses of hubris, calamities and pathos. For if we believe that it is they that are responsible for the allotted portion then we can only resign ourselves to the fact that all tragedy is preordained, inevitable. And so why bother writing about it? I don't know the answer to this question. But I must continue until the end of the trajectory. I have witnessed atheists pray to god or gods during junctures of great pain and suffering only to recant at a later date. But the intruder is not the story. He is just an example of fate. I will now relate to you my story.

It wasn't love. Love permeates the insular, so it was not love. Isabel MacCaffrey knew it wasn't love. But if it was love, love is reversible, it is not irrevocable. Having one's teeth pulled is binding. There was a young couple that experimented during coition, they moved with alacrity from toothpaste to cocaine. Everything was wonderful until they came upon a drug best omitted. How the drug found itself in the bedroom is a perplexing quandary, but I haven't the time or the energy to conjecture a mendacious trajectory. Suffice to say that during coition the drug was meted out and the teeth were pulled while both were in an iridescent nebula. Through false dentures the girl told the judge that her boyfriend was innocent and did not deserve to go to prison. Both were fined for wasting police time. And so brushing her teeth and staring into the mirror at her reflection, Isabel MacCaffrey knew it was not love, but if it was love so be it.

There are two things that I have read that are of interest to me concerning Marcel Proust; the first thing is that he was an inveterate masturbator and the second that he received a letter from an American lady living in Rome. Supposedly the lady in question impugned Proust why it was that he was so verbose. When I read this I was startled for this impugning is still in animation. There is an endeavor even now that is slightly Orwellian of eradicating the adverb. It has been stated that by using the adverb one is too verbose, one overwrites, one is a poseur. Contemporaneous fashion dictates that one be concise, concrete in one's sentences. Fundamentally be an American. I have been told that one should only employ the word "said" when dealing with dialogue, that "bellow", "yell", and "exclaim" are both superfluous and ostentatious. There is even now at this moment around the world an emulation of American writing. I too have been guilty of writing about Amsterdam and 5th street. We all become quixotic with the New World, I suppose it is inevitable. I fear Calaban will have his day and devour the adverb omnivorously. So a warning is in call for I believe. I am guilty of overwriting, of being a poseur. I was talking to a lovely Belgian the other day and she was ebullient about adverbs, she had vim about words in general, she had this infectious love for words and it was through her love of words that buffed me up and now I am able to write the story of Isabel MacCaffrey.

So who was the love of Isabel MacCaffrey?

Chester Merril Daynes was a small boy who grew into a small man. His Mummy said that he would become a doctor. His Daddy said the Prime Minster. Anything was possible; all doors were open to Chester Merril Daynes. They doted on Chester Merril Daynes. He was handsome, he dressed ornately, and he was excellent at school. Everybody loved Chester Merril Daynes. He spoke Spanish, French and Latin. Chester Merril Daynes told Isabel MacCaffrey that he was a professional tennis player. He had twenty credit cards, ranging from golden to platinum. Chester Merril Daynes told Isabel MacCaffrey the reason he left University was because he was forced to play tennis professionally all over the world, Paris, Melbourne, New York. He was that good. Isabel MacCaffrey was blown away. Chester Merril Daynes was famous. Though she had to confess that she had never heard of Chester Merril Daynes before she met him in the pub. He bought her drinks though. Money was no object with Chester Merril Daynes. He was free and easy with his money. Chester Merril Daynes was rich.   Chester Merril Daynes dressed ornately. Chester Merril Daynes was famous. Chester Merril Daynes was handsome, though a little short for Isabel MacCaffrey's liking. Chester Merril Daynes' Mummy and Daddy loved him; they doted upon him. So she turned a blind eye to his displays of arrogant, haughty behavior. He was slightly supercilious, but so what? Her last boyfriend was violent. At the drop of a hat he would kick, punch, glass, stab anybody. The new boyfriend lacked empathy, he had a grandiose sense of self-importance, he was diminutive, that's all. It was how he compensated his size. He required excessive admiration; he needed mothering. Isabel MacCaffrey liked that, the last boyfriend was always missing, he only came round for a leg over. After he had deposited he left without a goodbye.

Isabel MacCaffrey had never been to Jamaica. That's where he was taking her. He set it all up; they were going to fly to Jamaica. She was over the moon. She had never been to Jamaica. She had never left the country. He had booked a five-night stay in the Presidential Suite. Isabel MacCaffrey couldn't believe her luck. He had shown her pictures of the Suite on his high-tech, expensive, diminutive laptop. He got the high-tech, expensive, diminutive laptop when he bought the MG motorcar; and the clothes; and Isabel MacCaffrey's new clothes. The night of the shopping they stayed at a fancy hotel. He never tried it on. He just showered, brushed his teeth and fell into a deep sleep. She had showered, brushed her teeth and laved. When he came out of the bathroom, he pulled back the sheets, said goodnight, climbed into bed and fell into a deep sleep. Isabel MacCaffrey was slightly disappointed. She couldn't wake him. He had stipulated that once asleep he was not to be rudely awoken. He proscribed all movement in the bed once he was asleep.

I blame my older sister. When I was five and extremely delicate, illness was forever plaguing me. I was effete, precarious, weak. I came upon one of her art books. The book had been left fragrantly open and my eyes landed upon Hogarth's *Gin Lane*. It was like coming upon the opened box of Pandora. My insular world was invaded by this gruesome image. I was raped, pillaged, eviscerated by the image before my eyes, like a teenager that loses her hymen, like a youth that is temulent for the first time. I could never go back. The macerated sot, the doxy dropping her helpless baby, surely the ramification of the fall would be death, preoccupied with her stuff, the man hanging himself, the grotesque, the grimaces, the gargoyles, the fighting, the drinking, the whoring suddenly became animated and elucidated, the reek, the deleterious odors filled my pink little nose, the noises, the screams, the bellows, the cusses penetrated my virgin ears. The siccity of my childhood was soaked in gin. I suddenly and incongruously found myself in a state of inebriation and like the child from the drunken mother's arms I fell.

Isabel MacCaffrey's father one night coughed. He sat up and coughed again and was dead. Isabel MacCaffrey had three sisters and three brothers. They all lived in a three-bedroom house. The house was small. She once had four sisters and four brothers but the twins were run over by a lorry on its way to the city. The manifest was chickens. It was a bloody mess. Her mother was a catalogue of misdemeanors. She had been molested, raped, beaten, knocked out, but she somehow had survived.

It was only after Isabel MacCaffrey went to work that she began wearing new clothes. Isabel MacCaffrey began smoking when she was twelve. Isabel MacCaffrey puked the first time she drank cider. Isabel MacCaffrey was not a tease. Isabel MacCaffrey didn't mind going down on boys. Isabel MacCaffrey secretly enjoyed it. There was a feeling of power being on her knees. Isabel MacCaffrey never loved any of the boys she had sex with. Sometimes she slept while they pumped her. She liked one boy, his name was Frank O'Keefe. Though he fell off the roof of the local church, he was up there stealing lead. They had to scrape him off the gravestones.

Isabel MacCaffrey didn't like working. Isabel MacCaffrey sold shoes at a shop in the city center. After work sometimes she went out with a friend, she would get drunk and find herself in the morning in a strange bed. Isabel MacCaffrey could not believe that Chester Merril Daynes wanted to take her out; she could not believe that Chester Merril Daynes wanted to spend money on her; she could not believe.

Chester Merril Daynes was going to take her to Jamaica.

John Webb was a drunk. He had punched Isabel MacCaffrey in the mouth. The punch dislodged a tooth and Isabel MacCaffrey's mouth overflowed with blood. She had to go to the dentist. John Webb was a big man. His body was covered with a myriad of amateur tattoos. A scar ran down the middle of his shaven head. He didn't like to watch the television. He didn't take Isabel MacCaffrey to the movies, ice-skating, dancing, picking flowers, on country walks and he never took her to Jamaica. He never spent a penny on Isabel MacCaffrey. Lunting, spitting, cussing and drinking he could be found down The Ship. Everybody said hello, gave a nod, a wink, a drink to John Webb. He slapped a few people here and there. He put young Philip MacIntyre in the hospital. Philip MacIntyre's eyes were never the same; the doctor said strabismus. Tell the tit I'll fix those eyes for him, proclaimed John Webb lifting a bottle into the smoky air. John Webb fucked Isabel MacCaffrey standing up or like a dog. He pulled her hair, he slapped her arse, he penetrated her anus with his thumb, he sometimes sodomized her. But he was not queer he proclaimed obstreperously. When he did this he never hit her. He never talked to her. She was invisible. Everything was going fine when one day a stranger walked into The Ship. The stranger located John Webb lunting, spitting, cussing and drinking. The stranger walked calmly over to John Webb and hit him over the head with an iron bar, right on the scar. The next day the landlord of The Ship said everybody could have one free drink for that bastard John Webb was dead.

The stranger was Alex Blackwell. One night he arrived home incongruously. He felt ill. The speed had hit a bad patch. He did the late shift at the cake factory. Alex Blackwell was shocked to hear his wife being fucked. Alex Blackwell surreptitiously tiptoed up the stairs. Stairs that he would normally run up, cheering, farting, swearing. When he got to his bedroom, through the open bedroom door Alex Blackwell witnessed John Webb sodomizing his wife upon his disheveled bed. Alex Blackwell had never sodomized his wife. Alex Blackwell was not queer he proclaimed obstreperously. Alex Blackwell saw a smile upon his wife's grimace.

All The Ship's locals went to the funeral. Isabel MacCaffrey was lachrymose. Jenny Blackwell was lachrymose. Alex Blackwell was eating sausage rolls in his prison cell.

John Webb's three brothers were all killed shortly after the funeral. One was taken up into the moors in a van and beaten to death with cricket bats. The other brother was shot while fucking a prostitute. He was down a backstreet up against a wall with his pants around his ankles. He never saw the killer. The police found him next morning with the prophylactic still on his cock. The third brother was handed some dodgy heroin. The injection was his last. They found him on the toilet. Before he croaked it he shat out his guts. Once eviscerated his heart exploded. His father found him and hung himself after drinking a full bottle of whiskey. They shipped the mother off to mental hospital.

Two days after the funeral Alex Blackwell surreptitiously

sneaked duct tape into his cell, with the duct tape he wrapped his sheets round until the sheets were bound tightly into a rope, next he moved his bunk, he tied the rope around the bars in the window and hung himself.

It was not long after this terrible effrontery that Jenny Blackwell went to the doctor believing she was pregnant with the child of John Webb and found out she had instead a cancer. The tumor was made up of teeth, hair, bone, marrow and even an undeveloped vitreous orb. This benign monstrosity was quickly cut out of her, but whereas this tumor was benign, she was indeed riddled with a malignant cancer. She was black on the inside. She passed away with much celerity once the news spread throughout the estate.

Chester Merril Daynes lived in mansion, thought Isabel MacCaffrey. It was not a mansion, though it was a six-bedroom house. The driveway went on and on, but the MG zoomed across the gravel with ease. Their garden was blooming with pink, red and white roses. Isabel MacCaffrey was inebriated with the odors, the swirling trees, and the vortex of colors. There was no hint of gray, cement, concrete or plastic flowers.

The Merril Daynes' home was a home to die for. Nobody lived on top of them, there would be no sound of shoes banging against the wall, no reek of next door's piss, no barking dogs, no dirty children, no decomposing junkies, no moaning johns, no lip from prostitutes. Isabel MacCaffrey sighed deeply, no pervert spying upon her. Once she climbed out of the bath and there was the next-door neighbor with his cock in his hand. She nearly fainted. She stood there catatonic. The neighbor shot and fell to his death. The drainpipe gave way. It had rained a lot that year.

Make yourself at home, bellowed Chester Merril Daynes from the kitchen.

He was busy fixing up a few cocktails, he had told her.

Cocktails! Isabel MacCaffrey could not believe the stratum she had penetrated. The wallpaper was cerulean said Chester Merril Daynes. Isabel MacCaffrey saw a deep blue.

This will abirritate over your ruffles, said Chester Merril Daynes, handing Isabel MacCaffrey a funny shaped glass. A gage d'amour!

Isabel MacCaffrey knew not to grimace, to manifest perplexity, she knew that Chester Merril Daynes would not hit her, but still he would explode. It was too good to mess with.

Isabel MacCaffrey felt uncomfortable in the leather, she wouldn't place the glass upon the table and she was worried that there was mud on her shoes. Chester Merril Daynes kicked his shoes off, lit a cigarette, flicked the ash with abandonment, spilt his drink and talked endlessly about Jamaica, about himself, mostly about himself. The tennis was going jolly good, heaps of cash, lashings of fun. Chester Merril Daynes flashed out a twenty, lit the rolled up note and used the flame to light a cigarette for Isabel MacCaffrey. His loquacity, the ostentation, the flagrancy overwhelmed Isabel MacCaffrey. She told herself that she would fuck him, really fuck him. She knew he had never been fucked and she knew that she would fuck him like he had never been fucked before.

She fucked William Stores. She really fucked him. He played for the local football team. He wouldn't stop calling her. She sucked his cock. He used to send flowers. She rode him. He sent chocolates. But one night Webb nearly decapitated him. He never called after that night. They were in the casino and winning when suddenly from behind Webb appeared with a stool.

Mummy and Daddy are in Spain, Chester Merril Daynes informed Isabel MacCaffrey. They will be gone for a few weeks. The darlings do it every now and again, to get away from the hurry, the crowds, the city.

Chester Merril Daynes discerned worry within Isabel MacCaffrey's countenance. Chester Merril Daynes liked the simple ways of Isabel MacCaffrey, and with a bit of polish she wouldn't be that out of place within his society, though obviously always one step below him. Chester Merril Daynes knew that if he telephoned Isabel MacCaffrey at one in the morning she would arrive at ten past one. Chester Merril Daynes liked the fact she didn't understand Spanish, French and Latin. Chester Merril Daynes found a pleasure that Isabel MacCaffrey left school without a hint of education. Isabel MacCaffrey didn't even know what a pronoun was, or that Shakespeare was a Catholic. Chester Merril Daynes loved to hear her puerile giggle, he loved to hear her jejune conversation; he loved answering her fatuous questions. But Chester Merril Daynes didn't love Isabel MacCaffrey, even though she ostensibly, no, obviously, loved Chester Merril Daynes.

I need the bog, emitted Isabel MacCaffrey overcome with pusillanimity.

The restroom dear, corrected Chester Merril Daynes superciliously. When we are in Jamaica you must say restroom. Don't forget we are the civilized ones. We can't manifest any kind of weakness to the blacks dear.

Sorry! replied Isabel MacCaffrey, lowering her head.

I will let you off this time, answered Chester Merril Daynes seriously.

Where are the restrooms? emitted Isabel MacCaffrey diffidently.

Where are the restrooms, dear? said Chester Merril Daynes slowly losing his patience.

Where are the restrooms, dear? propitiated Isabel MacCaffrey with tears looming behind her lids.

That's grand! roared Chester Merril Daynes blooming, his countenance effusing with a deep crimson. Use the bog upstairs, I don't want to hear you pissing and shitting!

His laughter was a brouhaha.

She told herself that she would fuck him, really fuck him. She knew he had never been fucked and she knew that she would fuck him like he had never been fucked before.

Jamaica.

Mummy and Daddy in Spain.

The twenty credit cards, the mobile telephone, the MG, the mansion, the intoxicating garden, the high-tech, expensive, diminutive laptop.

John Webb had punched Isabel MacCaffrey in the mouth. The punch dislodged a tooth and Isabel MacCaffrey's mouth overflowed with blood. Isabel MacCaffrey had to go to the dentist.

At the top of the stairs Isabel MacCaffrey realized she had not asked which of the hundred doors led to the restroom. The landing went on and on with doors, fine prints in wooden frames, pictures in black and white and in colour. Small fictitious chandeliers illuminated the landing. Isabel MacCaffrey didn't know which door to open. She was overcome with fear; she did not want to upset Chester Merril Daynes. She wandered aimlessly up and down the landing. She couldn't make up her mind. She was lost in her trepidation. She needed to pee, she knew she had to be downstairs for Chester Merril Daynes; he would explode if she was missing for too long. Isabel MacCaffrey stopped before a door. It was potluck she knew. She prayed, but not to god.

Where the bloody hell are you? bellowed Chester Merril Daynes cantankerously.

Isabel MacCaffrey pushed open the door.

Daddy was prostrated face down upon the disheveled bed. What was incongruous was that his left foot was missing. It wasn't hidden under a blanket or a sheet; it was missing. The sheets were gold and black and extremely expensive. The foot was no longer connected to the left leg. It had been hacked off. The foot was nowhere to be seen. The blood had coagulated, dried and flaked away. Isabel MacCaffrey looked into the hollow darkness of the aperture. It was an impenetrable darkness. Isabel MacCaffrey followed a trajectory over the undulating mess upon the bed; her eyes journeyed slowly over a missing right ear and a lacuna in the head of the ostensibly dead Daddy. Daddy had been bald. Isabel MacCaffrey impassively looked upon the hands that were missing their fingers; the arms that had been broken and twisted incongruously; her eyes wandered aimlessly and landed inertial upon a foreign object that was protruding from Daddy's anus. Isabel MacCaffrey winced for she knew what it was like having something uncomfortable lodged up her arse. In her peripheral vision there was a fulguration. Isabel MacCaffrey went with alacrity to the source and saw upon the floor Mummy half-naked with legs akimbo. Mummy's head was rested upon an ornate pillow. There were manifestations of necrophilia. Isabel MacCaffrey drew a correlation with Mummy's position on the floor for she would lie just like that on those dark nights in the park when she would let snotty nose teenagers pump her for all they were worth, but she never had the pillow. Her eyes darted between the bed and floor until she developed strabismus.

Isabel MacCaffrey shut the door. She rubbed her eyes. She shook her head. She needed to pee. Isabel MacCaffrey walked down to the next door and opened it. It was the rest room. Light flowed into the room from a window above the bathtub. Isabel MacCaffrey was profoundly impressed. This was style, the bather could watch the clouds float by and even from the toilet one could see the sky. Isabel MacCaffrey rolled toilet paper around her hand and placed the roll into the bowl atop of the water to deaden the sound of piss hitting the water. She turned on the water taps also. Isabel Mac-

Caffrey didn't want Chester Merril Daynes to hear the piss hitting the water. Chester Merril Daynes would not be happy if he heard her urinating. Isabel MacCaffrey sat upon the toilet and urinated. She looked up and watched the clouds sail by. It was like taking a piss in the park after the snotty nose teenagers came inside of you. She always forced herself to piss afterwards.

Where have you been my dear? asked Chester Merril Daynes, sounding exasperated by Isabel MacCaffrey's long absence.

On the toilet? answered Isabel MacCaffrey, sounding vague; it was as though there was nothing behind those petite lips, those almond eyes.

You didn't disturb Mummy and Daddy did you? asked Chester Merril Daynes with an air of frivolity. They're in need of their beauty sleep.

No! uttered Isabel MacCaffrey, still not sure what she came upon.

A dream. A chimera.

You couldn't disturb them! bellowed Chester Merril Daynes facetiously waving his cocktail glass and lunting cigarette. They're dead the fuckers!

An erudite American, a wonderful writer, informed me of the peripatetic facial mole on Albertine's beautiful countenance. Was this deliberate I wanted to impugn. How could such a mistake slip through? We discussed rather verbosely and undoubtedly with much tedium about the etymology of the word transvertebration, but I forgot to ask him why Francoise manifested so much rage when she slit the chicken's throat. And this now gets me thinking about the time Isabel MacCaffrey was raped in the backstreet. John Webb punched her to the floor and grabbed her dress and stripped her. Upon the wet ground he took her, she screamed loudly, beat him with her fist until she was fatigued, she cried and begged for mercy and this brings me to how John Webb cried as the blood bubbled from the laceration across his throat. His weeping was analogous to that of a five year old boy seeing for the first time Hogarth's *Gin Lane*.

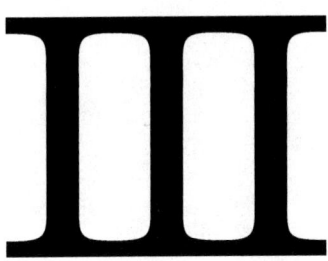

THE FOOL

KERZ: MID-SEASON TRAINING

joe shooman

Ahhhhhhhhhhhhhhhhhhhhh shit the train's gone without me 'cause I've been back home at the footy and on the beer and DD's been plying me with cheap Aldi Vodka all afternoon and instead of going for a curry I've had to risk limbcrushing horror in the queue for the ticket which I hold that has my fate down in spades and which means I have to go back to the Pool when all I wanna do is hang round with the rest of the moidering crazyheads and drink till I can't talk any more and have a double in every pub in Upper Bangor then head downtown for a quick one in the Firkin then back to the Belle Vue and two pints decked at last orders then a Donner Kebab from Mo's and with grease and chili running down my immaculately anaesthetized chin shout suavely at the stupid goddamn gorgeouslegged fatarsed hickslags tottering out of the ffycin Octagon then I'll walk back with me lads all the way to Ralphie's House for more bitterlagerportwhatever'sleftinthehouse, vicious arguments, losses at Playstation, softcore pornography and a 5AM sick in the shower if I can make it that far from my shivercouched cerebruination.

But nnnnnnnnnnnno, these days things are different, and because I'm mature ha ffycin ha and have Important Things To Do Tomorrow in another country I need to Be Strong and anyway if I missed one train, well, ffyc it, doesn't matter cos there's another 'un in 45 minutes, I'll get that instead and spend the interimtime on double brandies in the Station Hotel as is required of me, otherwise I'll start to get a hangover and I hate getting hangovers when I'm on trains it makes me feel sick so I'll phone up I'll phone up yeah yeah I'll phone up Lise, she'll have a drink with me and maybe maybe she'll make me stay here and help me avoid the weeks months years of Real And Important Work I got ahead and help me rediscover the doledragging days that are only notable for their interchangeability and the world can wait for me for a change. HA!

Aaaaaaaaaaaand Lise comes and we have a giggly Martini and singalonga S Club 7 on the jukebox and flirt as per usual and as per usual skirt round the wider topic of how-why-did-it-never-quite-happen-for-us, then with incredible timing and through my smudgy eyes I espy the new train pull in and as per usual get a surge of piquant nostalgia as she gives me a hug and looks me in the eyes and tells me "How did we get to be so far apart?" but the words that actually come out are "Have yourself some fun in the Big City and maybe me and Rhys will come up in a few weeks, eh?" and so I do get on the train, staggering wildly with dirty washing in dirty holdall holstered across dirty Holstened torso.

And I roll a cigarette and lean out the door which is still open because we ain't due to leave for another 10 at least minutes and I wave Lise away with a blown kiss and a wink and she enjoys it as much as I as we both know I'm loving the movement of her shoulders in her army shirt as she is reclaimed by the city of my birth, and at the very last point that we can still possibly see each other properly she almost turns round as is right and as is also right she walks on and out of sight as I finish my cigarette and swig mightily from the bottle of Coke and Vodka that I've had the foresight to prepare by lifting it from DD's pocket when he was celebrating Bangor's second goal.

Sooooooo I spit out the fagend and almost fall out the train tryna volley the mythaffycar into the distance but it slides off me dirty trainer and disappears underneath the wheels of me homewagon.

Time to find a seat so I start walking up the train expecting a few tables filled with some life and maybe some stagnight pissheads on their way from Dublin to the Pool that I can maybe laugh at behind my seat and at very very best have a drink with and listen to stories and tell em lies of my own but it seems I'm the only one in the back carriage and I don't want to be alone with my vodka and my thoughts and my mind's racing with the night I'm missing, the nights I've missed since I moved and became old and sensible instead of young and insensible so I, carrion, carry on walking up the aisle to the second carriage where there's undoubtedly gonna be someone I can sing to in silence and who can help me imagine it's better to go forward than stay back for a stayback in one of the local pubs in which I've spent thousands of pounds, hours and braincells over the years.

But nobody here either so I whistle as I resign meself to tomorrows lost and tomorrows yet to come, and it echoes somewhat messily round the emptiness. Jamie Oliver-lipped with countless lagers as I am, insodoing I manage to flobspit all over my replica footy shirt, try and wipe it off with my hand that's covered in ash, and make a right ffycin bollox of that as well. So I laugh and wander up the train to the last carriage. Which turns out to be completely empty too and I'm wondering whether I can get off and go for another brandy but then I'd maybe miss this one as well and anyways I've made the decision to go Where I Now Must Call Home so the old and sensible thing to do is to stay onboard and just find a seat and read the Star if I can find a way to stop the words flying about the carriage and make sense of the blurred pictures of some bloodboilingly unattainable lissom wannabes pouting and preening in their bra and pants.

Weeeeeellll look at this there's nobody here all these tables and chairs and that and any seat I want, that's cool I guess. And here too the driver's door open to his cockpit, that's cool.

Massive swig all but makes me puke there and then, and because I manage to hold it down and the retching is only dry though the stomach is a tight ball of terror, I'm filled with dunderheaded dreams of glory and I can see Bangor's winning goal hit the net as I pop my head round into the cockpit fully expecting a boot in the face or a Get Th' Ffyc Out Of Here and a slammed door.

Ffyc me look at this it's like friggin Star Trek in here all the dials and buttons and stuff, that's well cool, and you can see all the way into the tunnel right up to the corner! Excellent. Ooops bit of a stagger there young Kerz gotta watch that. Ah sod it let's take the weight off then at least I can say I've sat in the driver's seat for a change! Ha ha. Pretty comfortable chair this, wonder if it turns round. Smart! Does a bit. Wow the view here's top class, can see either side too and look at the cars there coming underneath the railway bridge. Ha this is ffycin ace imagine if I really was the ffycin boi in charge of this mother, pretty hard job when you think about it tryna keep this baby on them thin bits of metal ha ha ha. Would be good to get home though would be top class, where the ffyc is everybody? Bastards all gone for a curry then out on the piss and I won't get back till 9 at least cos I gotta ffycin 45 minute bastard wait in Chester and then gotta getta taxi to me house and shower and change and all that stuff so that's like 10 maybe half 10 before I even see the inside of another pub and god knows where all the Pool pissbastards will be by then might not even see anyone I know unless I can get there sharpish.

That really is fabbbbbbbbooooooooo the way them tracks sorta get closer together in the tunnel, nice one. Just like on TV, ffyc it, where is everybody sod it we need to start getting off soon gotta catch the lads before they decide to go to probably ffycin Concert Square, instead of I dunno the Jacky cos at least you can hear what people are saying in there then maybe onto Liquidation if we can be arsed with it but if we don't get there soon I'm gonna be on me own and wandering round chasing em and I don't wanna do that no chance kidda. Ffyc it what do all these dials mean? Can't be that much to work out it's only gotta be stop and go hasn't it? All the ffycin driving's done with signals and that surely, gotta be a piece of piss, innit?

Ffycin starved now mate. Hoold up there boi gotta pie in me bag I think ffycin superb where's that bastard whooooooooooooooooo fall outa chair BONK BONK BONK ON THE HED onto the floor crawlin about in the cockpit here's my bag open it YESSS!!! Let's get back up steady Kerz back inta your chair that turns round a little ffyc it watch the crumbs wipe em off the dials and buttons and shit oops there goes some gravy ffyc wipe that off we gotta go in a mo where the hell is everybody? Sick of this now sod it we could be at Rhyl at LEAST by now if we'd gone when I got on this bastard and how hard can it be to drive it anyway if we don't go soon I'm gonna get off and I'll be able to catch Lise and tell her once and for all that, well, whatever I should of three years ago when it was easier ah ffyc it bite the pie ahhhhh now THAT is gorgeous that is let me put it down here and wipe me hands ffycin bastards are well gonna be in Baa Baas or somewhere and I won't be able to get in there unless we get goin pretty sharpish one of these ffycin buttons has gotta make it go, how hard can it be? Ffyc it this must be something reeeeeeeach for the stars I can see a good 50 yards ahead so ffyc it we should be in Rhyl anyway bastards nobody on here but me let's get this goddamn shooooooow on the road well not a road but ha! Climb every mountain hiiiigh an REACH! Nah that don't do much bugger bugger what bout this one turns round a bit nope dials are moving a bit maybe maybe that's me head ha ha ha ah what a cool view look at the cars matey all rushing off and I got a whole clear track won't even stop in stations do the whole thing in 30 mins I reckon all the way to Chester why stop? Ffyc it! Gotta be a start button or summat here somewhere hasn't there? Otherwise it's half TEN for ffyc's *sake what bout this red bastard* BEEEEEEEEEEEEEEEEEEEEEEEEEEEEEEEEEEP *oops not that one obviously ah shit ffycin hell ffycin hell ffycin hell me pie's fallen this bastard ain't movin sod it better have that back let's go hunt-the-pie ha ha ha careful as you go me old matey bend down ooooooooooo oooopsie Bumperoo on the floor again ffyc it ha ha ha gotcha ya cunt have a bite um what's that outa the corner of my eye ahhhhhh*

-Hi lads, I grin winningly through the squishy chewage

Therrrrrrrrrrrrrre's two of the buggers - a stressed-looking bloke in a semi-redcoat jacket with all pens in the top pocket, and a fat bastard mustachioed Train Rozzer - both standing in the doorway looking down at my mature, sensible and Important Things To Do Tomorrow personage all rolling about in the dust and grime on the floor of the driver's cab with me clothes and hands all covered in puff pastry and globules of processed meat of indeterminate origin and a ffyc-off grin on my face because I've got my pie back and germs don't count if it's on the ground for less than 2 seconds.

Sooooooooooo I surprise myself by standing up and not swaying more than say a ferry and getting my bag and almost pushing past the Rozzer and the redface redcoat Train Man bloke with me pie in me mouth and flopping down onto a seat by a table and whistling a shitfaced mixture of S Club and Match Of The Day and spitting crumbs all over them white hankies on the backs of the seats. But I'm absolutely astonished when I glance behind me to find that the Train Man's whisking over like he wants to smack me chops to China, closely followed by the Rozzer who's taken off his Rozzer hat and put it under his Rozzer arm.

Aaaand so I immediately get on top of the situation by whipping out me ticket and offering it to Train Man who seems to be trying to attract the Train Rozzer's authoritative attentions, and I swear Train Rozzer right behind him has shaking shoulders. I feel I should say something as Train Man stands staring at my outstretched ticket incredulous and in complete dumbfounded silence so I chime:

-Pie?

and offer a bite out of friendly banter. Train Man moves closer to me and I'm confused by now and starting even to fall asleep a bit and then Train Man looks at Train Rozzer almost accusingly so Train Rozzer draws himself up to Full Rozzer Height and nods at Train Man solemnly. All of a sudden I get one of them thar moments of clarity and realise that I could well be in deep shit here, having but for the Grace Of Ginsters almost hijacked a ffycing train and if it weren't for The Slippage Of Pie, by now I could've and probably would've ploughed the multi-tonned bastard into the back of a less-drunk vehicle, some cows, a station or worse and by ffycin Christ it just don't bear thinking about kidda. So no doubt Train Man and Train Rozzer are planning on grappling me to some radiator or other and beating the living clonk out of me in justified retribution and then I'd be in cuffs and off to Chester with free Rozzerlike accommodation and later a nice trip down to Risley so I'd be stuck in Merseyside anyway and my eyes spin as I look at Train Man and he seems to be urging Train Rozzer to get this ffycin idiot sorted out and where he belongs behind ffycing bars not in them the pissed up twat.

Ooooh ffyc I'm in the shit now.

And as Train Man moves away with puffed out belly at a Superbly Handled Situation, slamming and locking the door of his cockpit with tremendous and supercilious finality, Train Rozzer musters up his full Rozzerness and twitches his moustache at me.

Ooooh ffyc.

Train Man starts the engine and we begin to lurch forward

to Chester and custody. My brain racing at the loss of liberty and horrendously aware of my mashed-up mind and alcohol-battered body, I start to feel dangerously contrite and panicky, and I can taste pie-and-vodka flavoured bile every time I breathe out. S Club 7 runs through my head, but now the nursery-rhyme shaMotown is a mocking and dismembering jumble of junkyard jeering. I start to sweat and I need a piss, but I can't move because I don't want to make things worse than they are.

Ffyc ffyc ffyc ffyc ffyc ffyc ffyc ffyc ffyc ffyc ffyc ffyc ffyc ffyc ffyc…

Train Rozzer sits himself down right opposite me and looks me up and down for a full ten seconds.

As we gather pace and rhythm and the trees merge into an ectoplasmic mulch outside the windspeeding windows, Train Rozzer starts to fiddle with his pen and notebook. He plonks his Rozzer hat on the table between us, turns down the chattering of his Rozzer Radio in his Top Train Rozzer Pocket, breathes deeply, and finally speaks:

-Is that a Bangor City shirt?

-Er…

-Yeah thought so, I used to be goalie down there in the 70s, Jimmy Conde, George Morton, whatshecalled Tony Broadhead, what a team we had, suppose you're too young to remember, but…

We shake hands and say fond goodbyes at Shotton.

I've still got his autograph on the back of me ticket.

THE IMMUTABLE LAWS OF PHYSICS

eric jones

Four men embarked from the dock at nearly four in the morning: a butcher, a pastry chef, a brick mason, and a chandler. They shoved off in a great wooden tallow tub, which was the chandler's from the butcher by arrangement. The tide ponderously drew them out from the pier, past broken down craft tethered to rickety, rope-hung docks. They were drunk, of course, to be in a wooden tub at that hour, and soon clear out of bleary sight of land.

This meant nothing to their mirth. They laughed and told mendacious fish tales of faulty misdeeds till the rising gray declared an overcast day. It was then that the pastry chef made a curious observation.

"That's unusual," he said rather plainly.

"What's unusual?" the butcher asked.

The pastry chef wrinkled his nose and pointed. "That patch of water, way off over there. It's caught on fire."

The chandler, fancying himself a bit more experienced with fire declared, "That's nonsense!" but when he looked he saw that it wasn't. "That doesn't make any sense."

The mason deliberately said nothing.

The butcher stood up, agitated, but the rocking of the tub he provoked urged him to sit back down again. "I've never known water to catch fire."

"There is something unique about it," the pastry chef admitted.

"Unique?" the butcher said, a bit frustrated, "Well, it just doesn't happen!" and he continued, muttering, "Water on fire, the very idea."

"Object all you want," the pastry chef returned, "but that patch over there is right aflame."

"Well, I think it's ridiculous and I won't be bothered by it anymore. I'm busy!" Though what the butcher was busy at in the small wooden tub not even the mason could fathom.

For a time they sat there thinking, till the chandler broke the silence. "That fire from earlier," he continued though the butcher shot him an evil look, "I've been watching it for a space now and I'm convinced it might be spreading."

They all looked then and it was quite plain that the fire was spreading very rapidly. The pastry chef added, "I tell you, that's not right. Water isn't flammable at room temperature."

"Well, its not room temperature is it?" the butcher bitterly snapped. "We're at sea for one, and there's quite an extra bluster this morning what's more."

"I was only conjecturing-"

"Oh, conjecture yourself overboard if you're going to be for that nonsense," the butcher rejoined.

"Hey, hey," the chandler interrupted, "that talk isn't in the spirit of our little affair, is it?"

The butcher frowned. "Well, I apologize. It's just I wasn't welcome to the idea of seawater catching fire at first, but now I must admit, it has me a bit on edge." He busily redoubled his efforts at whatever little thing he was up to.

The chandler, feeling pressure that this was his area, offered another explanation. "Maybe it's not the water but a bit of algae or driftwood on the surface."

The pastry chef nodded approvingly at that but then jumped on the bandwagon when the butcher said the theory lacked good judgment.

"It wouldn't be spreading that quickly at any rate," the mason finally spoke.

"Well, what do you suppose it is?" The butcher was quite upset.

The mason leaned in close. "I didn't want to say anything," he started, soberly, darkly, "but there is a secret formula for an oil that burns on the surface of the sea."

The pastry chef gave him a queer look. "What would be the purpose of that out here?"

The suspense broke and the mason threw up his hands. "Oh, you're right then," he said a bit bitterly, "I suppose the water is on fire."

"No need for condescension," the pastry chef warned, "I am just waiting for a sensible explanation."

The mason said, "Well if that water over there is on fire, I should deduce that the water around us is no less flammable." This set them to thinking.

"Well, I'm not about to hold a candle to the sun," the chandler began, but at that moment it became clear that the little thing the butcher had been about the whole time was packing a pipe to settle his nerves. He took a steady match to it and began to puff.

The other three clutched their heads in panic. "Dear God, put that out!"

The butcher looked at them with a puss and tapped the glowing embers off the edge of the tub.

LIKE A THIEF IN THE NIGHT

malon edwards

A little girl grew horns.

Jamie says he's going to ride his bike over there and look at her and he says I should come too. He says he's not scared to go alone or anything like that but the little girl would be a cool thing to see and I shouldn't miss out. He says she's had horns for three days now (today is the fourth day), ever since Jesus came back. Jamie says all she does is play by herself in her driveway with dolls and a miniature tea set. You can see her driveway the next street over if you hide in those bushes in front of the boarded up house at the end of our block. That's what Jamie says. But he says you can't see her horns from there. He wants to see the little girl up close and touch her horns with his finger to see if they are sharp and will make him bleed.

My uncle says the little girl is a child succubus, a devil spawn, the daughter of Satan, the Anti-Christ. He says if you shave all her hair off you'll see 666 in the back of her head. I wonder if those sixes are itchy and scabby like the ringworm I had last year.

I get my bike out of the garage and ride with Jamie toward the end of our block. It's a Huffy trick bike; Jamie says I should get a mountain bike so we can ride through the dirt trails in the forest preserve behind our houses but you can't jackrabbit too good with a mountain bike.

We ride slowly. At first, I wasn't going to go with Jamie. Watching the little girl from the bushes is okay with me. Jamie says I shouldn't be scared of her; we're her people, her followers. We won't explode and burst on fire from within if she looks at us.

I'm not saved. Neither is Jamie. Neither is my uncle. I've never been baptized. I believe there's a God, there's a devil, there are angels, there are ghosts, there are monsters and there are aliens. So does Jamie. So does my uncle. My uncle says that's all we need. He says we didn't need to go to church to hear how awful we were during the week; we were there when we were being awful so we already knew. My parents didn't want to push me to be baptized; they wanted me to make that decision on my own. I think if they knew Jesus was coming back this soon they would have made me and I would have been caught up in the rapture with them.

It's been real quiet for the past three days. No cars hardly drive down our street and Jamie and I are the only ones I've seen outside since Jesus came back. It's kinda hot, but not hot enough to keep people inside all day and all night. My uncle said it's because people are embarrassed. They don't want to come out of their houses because then people would see they didn't go with Jesus. The phone hasn't rang since He came back and all the television stations show snow. It's real boring. That's why I decided to go see that little girl with Jamie. I told my uncle that people like us shouldn't be embarrassed to go out because we knew Jesus wasn't coming for us. He said not all the people left are people like us. He also said that people like us are waiting. I asked for what but he didn't answer me.

Jamie and I are less than ten feet from the little girl. She's younger than us, probably four or five. Her horns are a dull whitish-gray and poke up through her short-cropped, straight red hair. She continues playing without looking at us, singing quietly to herself until our shadows fall on her. She doesn't have a shadow. She looks up at us and smiles. She is what we are waiting for. I don't smile back. I don't want to. I don't think Jamie will try to touch her horns.

SCRAMBLING

tom meek

Always wear a condom, even with your girlfriend. Go easy when hazing the freshmen, you never know who'll be covering your blindside for the home opener. Never talk back to the coach. Take that cocky shit from the black guys who make you look good when they streak down the field. Never be boastful to reporters. Floss. Always be polite to recruiters; treat each like they're the first. Try to stay in state. Don't go double A. Feed Ma each morning. Wash her sheets if necessary. Make sure Mrs. Vasquez gets her dinner while you're at practice. Call Tilson at the end of the month and remind him to send the money he likes to forget about. Stretch. Hit the weight room before lunch, but don't lose any flexibility in your throwing arm. Slide for first downs. Only dive headlong if the game's on the line. Never smash the mailbox of any of the boosters who pay for the Friday night lights—and never, ever, fuck one of their daughters, like Charles Ray did; he ended up with a busted kneecap and lost his scholarship to College Station. Don't get into fights with drunken has-beens, jealous wannabes and jilted boyfriends who'll always line up to take shots at you. If you get in a fight, take them out quick, but make sure your fist is packed right so you don't break a knuckle. Avoid knives. A slice, like the skewered spleen of your tight end who got into it with a jealous husband, can cost the season. Don't pack. A gun for anything but hunting can land you in a cement box. Cats and jackrabbits are fair game for off-road "Death Race," but dogs and armadillos are off limits, no matter how drunk you get. Never fumble a snap from center. Always place the ball firmly in the back's abdomen.

Don't get injured. Never pay for a lap dance at the Vixen Den, unless it's Daiquiri, aka Cheryl Ann Travis, the head cheerleader when you were a freshman, because she usually throws in a complimentary "State Championship" blowjob. Don't stare at Jenny Rodgers' tits at the bowling alley; her brother, a fourth round pick of the Rams, works the bar, carries a snub nose and still thinks she's a virgin. Never let your opponent back in the game. Never lose. Two losses in a season is a failure, two in a row has never happened, and if it does, nothing else will matter. Tell people they've got nothing to worry about when they ask you about the upcoming game with the Freemont Raiders even though they'll bring up the fourth quarter INT you tossed last year that gave them the game. Always outplay your backup in practice. Don't give coach fodder for contemplation. Eat at Skippy Jack's Drive-in when "Easy" Mary Ellen Henning is working; she used to go with Tilson when he was the starting H-back and she was the homecoming queen and throws you a cheeseburger on the house when Skippy's not around. Clean Ma up when you get home. Study the playbook. Put Ma to bed. Do your homework. Look in on Ma. Study the playbook some more. Get a good night sleep. Get Bs. Don't get caught cheating. Gas up at Dyson's; the old man lets you fill up for free so he can reminisce about his son who backed you up on JV, but then dropped out, joined the Army and caught a slug in Iraq. Be grateful to your linemen. Smile to parents when signing autographs for the Pee Wees. Pump fake in the pocket before rolling out. Hope the 'Horns come through with the full ride before the other bigs put the squeeze on you. Follow up with 'Tuky and Cal to see if they're serious about sending you home every other week. Don't throw over the middle unless you've checked off the safety. Put plenty of touch on the ball when leading your speed receivers. Win state. Remember where you came from. Be true to Ma. Get the fuck out of here.

SLUG LOVE

grant perry

My beer-sodden eyes followed the roll of Karen's hips as we mounted the steep flight of stairs to her maisonette. The stairs opened onto a hallway with doors to the left and right, leading to living room and kitchen respectively. My gaze was drawn to a further flight of stairs, which led to the bedrooms.

I followed Karen into the kitchen.

"Do you want anything to drink?" she asked.

"What've you got?"

"Well, I'm going to have some wine."

"You're getting very sophisticated."

"Thanks. It's Marie's, but she won't mind. Look, the lazy cow's left all our washing in the machine again. I'll have to hang it out or it'll start to get that horrible smell."

"Don't mind me. A woman's work is never done, eh?" Why did I feel compelled to make such predictable and facile comments, I wondered?

Karen began to empty the washing machine that crouched in the corner of the kitchen and was now hanging a collection of bras, pants and T-shirts on a creaky wooden clotheshorse. She looked up. "Did you say you wanted wine or not?"

"What colour is it?"

"I didn't realise you were a connoisseur. If you want some there's a bottle in that cupboard next to the fridge and you'll get glasses in the next one along."

"Are those yours?" I was pointing incredulously, and not a little excitedly, at a minuscule pair of black lacy knickers she was arranging over the clotheshorse.

"Do they suit me?" she asked, holding them suggestively to her hips. I imagined they would suit her lithe, trim body very will indeed.

"Are they yours?" I repeated.

She gave me a withering look. "They're Marie's."

"Bloody hell! I knew she was a bit of a goer, I didn't know she was into stuff like this though." I had met Karen through Marie, who had had brief flings with a couple of my mates. Like Karen, Marie attended the Art College.

"'A bit of a goer?' That's the kind of thing my dad would say. They're just a pair of knickers."

"Only just! What about these ones?" I plucked a pair of worn, yellow cotton pants from the clotheshorse.

"They're Marie's too. And I don't think she'd appreciate you pawing and drooling over her underwear."

"You never know."

"You've not got some sad knicker fetish have you?"

"No more so than the next man. Why don't you hold up random pairs of knickers and I'll try to guess if they're yours or Marie's? We can move on to the bras after that." Was this playfully raffish repartee, or was I behaving like an arsehole?

"Why don't you just get on with opening that wine?"

By the time I had found the wine and a couple of glasses Karen had finished hanging up the washing.

"Have you had anything to eat?" she asked.

"Not really. I was just heading home for tea when I bumped into you."

"You can make yourself a sandwich if you like."

"I'm alright."

Producing a corkscrew from a drawer, she twisted it expertly into the neck of the bottle and eased out the cork. She handed the bottle back to me and, with the glasses tinkling in one hand, she led me up the stairs to her bedroom. She flicked on a small bedside lamp that lit the room with a subdued orange glow, sat on the edge of the bed and began to pour the wine. Meanwhile I was examining a collection of half-finished canvasses and sketches piled up in a gloomy corner of the room.

"Don't look at them."

"Why not? They're good. I like this one." It was a picture of an old man in an old armchair, painted in browns and yellows and creams. He looked lonely and abandoned.

"Yeah, well you're drunk. They don't stand up to examination in the cold light of day."

"You reckon?"

"Come over here."

There was something in the tone of her voice that made me comply immediately.

I joined her on the bed. She had already finished off most of her wine and her lips were glistening wet. She handed me a glass, but before I had chance to drink she laid down on the bed, reached up, and grabbing my tie, pulled me on top of her. I tried to rest my glass on the floor, but heard it tip and spill softly on to the carpet.

Her lips were cold from the wine and as her tongue slid across mine I could taste its fruity acidity.

Unclothed on the bed, Karen's mouth traced over me. Her lips slow and soft as ripe slugs. No more words now, only sounds.

A violent white beam of sunlight cut through a gap in the sloppily drawn curtains, diffusing a cold, bright light around the room. The small bedside lamp was still on, its meagre glow pathetic and superfluous in the stark new day.

I had awoken early and was feeling unwell. Too much to drink, not enough to eat and too little sleep. Propping myself on one elbow I turned to look at Karen. With her head drooped to one side her face sagged lifelessly. Her mouth, relaxed in sleep, was slack and ugly. Her eyes were smudged and blackened with the debris of sleep and old mascara. Her breasts flopped over on one side, their mass strangely diminished, the nipples shapeless and pulpy. In sleep she looked vulnerable and plain, nothing like the vivacious girl of last night. Gently I tried to wake her, stroking her hair and brushing it carefully behind an ear.

Karen made a noise to signify she was awake and snuggled up to me. I lay on my back and she rested her head on my shoulder, her flat hand running over my stomach. She began to kiss me lightly across the chest. Her lips were dry and they chafed against my skin. She raised her face toward me, her eyes still closed. We kissed, our lips scuffing against one another. Mossy tongues, heavy with a sour glue of saliva, met in our mouths like punch-drunk boxers. Karen's hand moved lower and I felt myself stiffening in her palm. Drawing myself up, awkward and clumsy, I maneuvered myself on top of her and, using my hand to guide me, started to work myself in. She was hardly moist and it was some time before I began to move freely inside her. Our mouths disengaged and I started to kiss her ears and down her neck, but found the fetid slug trail from my own tongue disgusting. I buried my face in the pillows. With my whole weight resting on her, I began to pummel into the body beneath me. She placed a steadying hand on my hip, trying to control my pace. I moved faster, thrust harder.

Soon it was over and a sense of sadness that I couldn't easily account for began to overtake me. I had a nagging feeling that everything had been spoiled.

"That was a bit fast and furious wasn't it? You in a hurry or something?" Karen's good-humoured cajoling annoyed me. It felt inappropriate.

I was lying on my back again. "I've got an early start at work today."

"You never said." Her tone had changed. She sounded annoyed now and that irritated me still further. I rose up on the edge of the bed, examining the heap of clothes on the floor. "You're not going right now," she said. It was a challenge, not a question.

"I've got to go to work."

Karen leaned over and put her arm around me, stroking my stomach again and pressing herself into my back. "Go in a bit late."

I bent forward to extract a sock from the pile on the floor. She let go of me and sank back into the bed. Straight away I missed the warmth and weight of her breasts on my back. I turned around.

"Look, I've got to go to work."

She didn't return my glance. "You didn't mention anything about an early start last night."

"I didn't want to think about work last night." This at least was true. I turned away from her and began pulling on my trousers. One leg was damp from the spilt wine. I picked my shirt off the floor. It was creased and stank of nicotine.

"I've got to go now. I'll be late. We're always busy this time of the month. I'll call you."

"Spare me."

Her back was to me now. She had switched off the little lamp and was taking a cigarette from a packet on the bedside table. As I turned to leave my eyes rested momentarily on the stack of canvasses in the corner of the room.

"Bye," I said.

No reply.

Smoke dissipated into scrolling ribbons. A cigarette was turning to grey ash in the porcelain-white ashtray. I knew when I lit it that I didn't really want it. Seated at a formica-topped table in a foggy-windowed cafe, I was still feeling unwell. My throat was sore, I could feel my eyeballs moving in their sockets, my brain was throbbing and acid was bubbling in my stomach. I took a last slug from my cup. It was cold and the bitter coffee grinds stuck to my tongue. I scraped it with my teeth and swallowed, grimacing. The only other customer in the cafe was an elderly man in an olive green anorak whose face was a blank of numbed concentration as his thumbs twitched at an ancient Gameboy.

A waitress appeared and began wiping down the table next to mine. Her lips were a thin red line, her complexion flushed and blotchy. She looked grumpy. Maybe she had a hangover too. Her uniform was clean and pressed and looked brand new, only serving to highlight the terminal grime of her once-white pumps. I got up to leave. If I didn't get a move on I really would be late.

"I shan't be two minutes."
"S'alright, no hurry."

By the photocopier, I pretended to read one of the documents I was waiting to copy. I didn't know the woman using the machine and was keen to avoid an exchange of cordial banalities. She was wearing a powder blue jacket with lilac piping and a short lilac skirt that showed off her slender, orangey, perma-tan legs. Her dress-sense put me in mind of daytime TV presenters and I could tell that she must hold a senior rank in the company. I had noticed that as women progressed through the office hierarchy they began to dump the sober, business-like blacks, greys and navy blues from their wardrobe in favour of bright colours and jackets with lurid checks and trimmings. Sometimes I'd find it a pleasant diversion to imagine what the insides of these women's houses might look like— all flock wallpaper and statuettes, with four-poster beds swathed in acres of drapery. Not today. The hangover was getting worse, and the acid in my stomach had subsided to be replaced by a hollow, empty sensation that was making me nauseous. I was anxious about the events of that morning – how I'd mucked things up and why I'd acted as I did.

"Just about done," the woman in powder blue said, half-glancing over a shoulder pad.

Before I got the chance to use the photocopier, I was joined by Julie from HR, one of the nicest people I knew at the company, someone with whom I had little in common. Julie really seemed to enjoy her job.

"Hiya! Are you waiting to use the copier? Is it alright if I have a quick go first? I've just got a couple of these to run off."

"Go ahead," I said.

The powder blue jacket turned around. "Hiya, Julie! Congratulations! Let's have a look then!"

After the powder blue jacket had ooh-ed and aah-ed over the engagement ring the two women fell to talking about dates and arrangements. I was relieved to have a little breathing space before having to trade small talk with Julie.

The powder blue jacket had taken herself off and after a pregnant pause Julie turned from the photocopier. "How are things?"

"Fine. Same as ever really." I knew I should offer my congratulations on her engagement, but felt inhibited, being unable to match the gushing performance of the woman in the powder blue. "Yourself?"

"I'm so busy getting everything organized for the employee awards." Each quarter the company handed out awards to employees who had excelled against a number of criteria such as 'Indefatigability' and 'Vision'. In my two years with the company I had yet to receive a nomination. "There's so much to do. Booking the conference hall, arranging for the catering, preparing all the Powerpoint presentations.... There, all done."

"Thanks. Oh, congratulations on your engagement." Somehow this sounded forced and awkward, but Julie thanked me warmly and beamed a big, happy smile.

I took the first sheet of the document, placed it on the glass surface of the copier, closed the lid and adjusted the settings to make twenty copies. The flashing light inside the copier hurt my eyes. I turned from the machine as it began to spew out the pages. Leaning my backside against it, I watched the bustle around the office. It was a wearisome sight. I saw people speaking to plastic telephones, or gazing into flickering screens as their hands convulsed over keyboards. It was barely mid-morning but the lack of sleep, the hangover, the dry chemical breath of the machine and its hypnotic clunking and whirring left me exhausted.

As the machine churned out the final copy I turned and reached down to bundle the finished sheets together. In doing so my fingertips brushed the top copy. It was warm and smooth. I thought of Karen and of last night. I sighed, rubbed my eyes and set the machine to print one hundred extra copies. As it began to churn out the paper, head hung and eyes closed, I allowed my hand to dangle at the machine's side, each new sheet slewing softly past my fingertips. I was trying to imagine what it might feel like to be in love.

THE MOOSE HUNTER

dean baker

The hunter adjusted the sights on his rifle. The moose was less than a hundred yards off and breathing heavily, vapor coming from its mouth in clouds. The hunter had been tracking it for two hours and the moose was tired.

He was near enough now and on higher ground, looking down at his prey. The moose lowered its head and moved its shaking legs in the deep snow. It was two hundred yards from the tree line, extremely vulnerable in the open. This was what the hunter was waiting for.

He looked back down the scope and zeroed the crosshairs on the moose's right flank. His breathing calmed to a slow pace as he prepared for the shot, his finger curled around the trigger. Rifle steady, he breathed in, then exhaled and squeezed the trigger. There was a thump in his shoulder as the weapon recoiled.

The moose was jolted by the hit, a sting in its right side. It tottered, legs plodding in the snow, then fell sideways. The hunter lowered his rifle and pulled his cap down before getting to his feet. He pulled out a pair of powerful binoculars and surveyed the stricken beast on the slopes below. It was down but still breathing, puffs of breath visible from its mouth.

The hunter picked up his rifle and walked back to the Jeep. He started the big diesel engine, and it roared to life. Shifting the gears, he pulled away, the chains on the tires gripping the snow. Slowly, the hunter climbed down the snowy slope into the valley towards his prize.

He was flushed with excitement when he reached it. He climbed out of the jeep and took out his hip flask, taking a nip of whiskey. He then took off his thick gloves and pulled out his long bladed hunter's knife. It was cold. Damn cold.

The hunter knelt down beside the moose and located the tranquilizer dart. He swiftly incised it at the entry point, using his knife to loosen the skin and remove the barbed dart.

Pulling a small length of rope from his knapsack, he attached one end to the moose's huge antlers and retreated towards the jeep. He attached the end of the rope to the winch, which he operated to heave the beast off of its side into a more upright position. With some effort he managed to set the animal so it was straight, resting on its knees. He cut loose the winch. By now the hunter was very fatigued, sweating and breathing hard. He sat down on a snowdrift and rested, taking another hit from his hip flask. Once he'd got his breath back he then set to work.

Even though it was minus two degrees with wind chill he started to remove his warm snow jacket. The wind was icy around his neck as it became exposed. He then pulled off his woolen sweater, feeling the goose bumps rise on his chest and arms. His nipples stiffened with the cold as he unbuckled his belt and pulled down his trousers. He'd had the forethought not to wear any underwear.

With his trousers round his ankles, not to mention a rod-stiff erection, he waddled towards the rear of the motionless moose. Taking a kneeling position, he lifted up the short tail with his right hand and guided his twitching penis towards the moose's steaming cavity. He gave a grunt of satisfaction as he felt the warmth of the moose on his icy cold penis and clasped his arms around the moose's girthy frame. It felt so invitingly warm against the bitter cold.

Slowly he began to thrust, his arms holding on tight as his hips bucked back and forth and his now blue behind danced with the motion. His breathing became heavier, little puffs of steam rising from his throat with each thrust and groan.

He quickened his pace, slamming his groin into the beast's behind with vigour.

But suddenly he heard a noise that made his heart fill with dread. His thrusts ceased and his dick began to go limp.

"Hey, moose-fucker!" A voice called through a loud hailer, echoing off the mountains of the valley.

The hunter withdrew himself from the moose and rolled to his side, his trousers still around his ankles. He grabbed at them furiously, trying to locate his pistol. As he did so, a rifle shot smacked into the snow to his left. He rolled once more, making for the cover of a snowdrift before another shot caused an eruption of snow where he'd just been.

He frantically struggled with the holster of his sidearm.

The hunter should have been freezing, half-naked in the snow, but the adrenaline rush of mortal danger was keeping his mind off his body temperature. He popped his head above the snowdrift and tried to see where his attacker was positioned. He saw a faint muzzle flash and felt the force of the passing bullet as it smacked down in the snow. From the inaccuracy of the fire he knew his attacker was using open sights, no scope, and was a lousy shot. He popped his head up again and aimed a snapshot roughly where he'd seen the muzzle flash. He cursed loudly as he fired the pistol twice more.

Another shot rang out, which shattered the windscreen of the hunter's jeep, followed by a crackling declaration from the loudhailer on the overlooking ridge.

"I'm gonna kill that fuckin' moose, you lousy prick!"

The hunter felt fear grip his heart like a cold iron vice.

"No!!" he screamed, jumping up from behind the snowdrift. "Don't shoot!" he shouted, throwing his pistol down and putting himself in between the rifleman and the moose with his hands raised.

"You love a moose more than me? You...you fucking...miserable...limpdick moosefucker!" the voice screamed, an eerie echo resonating round the valley.

"Sean?" the hunter called, confusion on his face.

"Too right Sean, you fucking bastard. I followed you this time, you perverted fuck!"

"Sean listen, it meant nothing, it was just sex. I swear. Let's talk aboot this."

"Just sex? What are you saying?"

"I can't give it up, my dad and I used to do this when he was alive. We used to do this together. Father and son. It doesn't mean I don't love you any more. Put down the gun, you paranoid bitch."

"It's too late, Greg. It's over. I can't share you with a moose. If you can't love me then you can't live."

With that, a shot rang out. The moose hunter felt it whiz past his cheek. He spun as it flew past and grazed the moose's rump, which exploded in a spray of fur and blood. The beast was roused to its senses, and started to stagger to its feet in the deep snow. It turned round and saw the half-naked hunter. Disoriented and slightly spooked, the beast's natural defense mechanisms flew into action. It lowered its head and pointed its huge antlers in the hunter's direction. The hunter stood trembling, his trousers still round his ankles, as a very scared and aggressive moose prepared to charge. It began to trot forward, picking up speed. The hunter turned and fled, struggling to hold up his trousers in one hand, the moose pursuing him through the deep snow. The moose caught the hunter in the small of the back and knocked him down, trampling over him before coming to a halt. It stood breathing in the snow for a second before beginning to return towards the felled hunter for the final attack. Its hooves cut through the snow as it neared the stricken hunter, about to finish him off, when a single shot rang out and the moose stuttered its steps, stumbled and fell in a heap on top of the hunter.

By the time Sean had reached the pair in the valley, the moose was dead. The hunter was near death too, pinned beneath a ton of dead animal.

"Greg, I'm sorry. I didn't mean it.... Why a moose you, stupid fucking queen? We could have been happy. I love you Greg."

"I know..." were the dying words of the moose hunter as the snow began to fall.

WERNER SCHWAB

aryan kaganof

It's Charlie Manson's birthday. He offers Sammy The Shake a drink. Sammy asks for a double of whatever Charlie's having.

"No. Make that two doubles."

Charlie's amused by Sammy's lack of tact. After a while the alcohol has loosened them both up to the point where they could pass for mates. Charlie tells Sammy that he's just broken up with Cortado. That she was wonderful in bed but he felt the need to roam. His eyes glaze up. Sammy suspects that Cortado did the breaking up. Charlie Manson admits to treating Cortado shamefully in order to find out how much she loved him. If she really loved him. Then the truth spills out.

"She dumped me."

Just then Cortado bursts in to the Winston. She's come for Charlie Manson's birthday. She kisses him full on the lips. Her lips are juicy as are her ripe paps. She stares at Sammy The Shake frankly.

"What's it like to be famous?"

These things happen instantly. Only idiots "chat up" women.

Sammy suggests to Charlie Manson that they all move on from the Winston to a fabulous night bar on the Zeedijk called the San Francisco, which is open for an extra hour. They dash through the tedious Amsterdam rain. Cortado covers her head with her leather jacket, her melons stick out at the moon. The moon is impressed, as is Sammy. Cortado confesses to him that acting is her passion.

Charlie Manson sits in between Cortado and Sammy The

Shake. Sammy leans over Charlie and asks her to sit next to him. "The view's better." She does. Everything's clear now. She wants to punish Charlie. He needs to be punished. Sammy's a form of poison. What the hell, it's better than nothing. Charlie Manson leans over Sammy to his ex, who has ostensibly come out to "support" him on his birthday, warns her about Sammy The Shake's reputation.

Sammy sits out the drama in silence. Keeps on drinking the latest double that Charlie Manson has bought him. Sammy The Shake doesn't believe in competing, but he does know how to outdistance the opposition. His philosophy is "I love the opposition." He can dimly hear snippets of Charlie Manson's conversation. Phrases like "ambivalent powerlessness" and "totally psychotic vodka troll" mean little to him. He's not one for small talk. He never cares what people are talking about.

Suddenly Charlie Manson stands up. He looks dizzy. Has downed one too many doubles this happy birthday party. He gives Sammy The Shake his hand which is weak, he lacks grip, has lost his grip of the situation, of his ex, the melon queen Cortado. He says goodbye to her. "I'll call you tomorrow." Hesitates. Hoping for her to join him. She stays put. Charlie Manson moves on, broken, looks back. "Sleep well, I love you."

Once her ex has disappeared, Cortado's breasts start growing. At 5am the lights come on. They walk out together. All is natural. It's a long walk to Amsterdam East. Sammy The Shake says nothing. Cortado doesn't stop telling him about the new German theatre and how fulfilling it is to get up on stage and go through meaningful dialogues with her soul. Indeed.

Upstairs in her third storey apartment she raises misgivings. Sammy the Shake takes off his boots and stretches out on the sofa while she lists her misgivings into his ear and then directly, tongue to tongue. She has so many misgivings and Sammy The Shake swallows them all. Naked, inside her, the misgivings still roll off her presses. Then she jumps out of bed and runs into the kitchen, hides under the table, sobbing broken misgivings.

Sammy moves to the toilet for a much-needed shit, understands everything when he sees Cortado's name on a poster advertising a play by Werner Schwab. She's rehearsing, her Schwabian mode. He tears off the piece of the poster with her name on it and wipes his ass. He closes the toilet without flushing and is careful to leave the shit-stained paper with her name on it on top of the toilet seat.

He goes back to the kitchen, scoops up her crying body and ploughs it into the bed. Her legs fold back effortlessly. He's excited when he places both feet flat onto the wall behind her. He pushes her toes into her face while her cunt screws itself tightly around his hardness. Then it's the misgivings again and Cortado starts crying that she doesn't want to.

She's weeping wildly now, crying that she's the "most awful woman ever". Sammy The Shake cannot help wishing that she would contain her rehearsals to the time spent in the theatre. It really is all too much. But he must come now.

He wraps her in a blanket, makes a cup of tea, mouths a string of inane platitudes meant to soothe her. When she's ready to go back on her back he knows he must pump it quickly, do his stuff and get away from this Schwabian horror. When he's nearly there she urgently whispers that he mustn't come inside her.

"What about in your mouth?"

"NO!"

She's horrified. Thick globs of it land on her lovely smooth belly. The play acting and the denial and the reality all collude at the interstices of the real and unreal. Then the phone goes. Of course it's Charlie Manson. Cortado bursts out sobbing, "Charlie darling something awful has happened…" Sammy nips out of the bed and gets all his gear on by the time Charlie's thrown the phone down and she's called him again.

"Why are you calling him?"

Cortado turns to Sammy The Shake, eyes icy with hatred. "Because I love him!"

HELP ME, I'M HUNGRY
jeff t. kane

Water blue and cloudy and pieces of light break up like glass on surface.

Arn Sharcarnahan swims in abandoned part of ocean with Eelio.

He is hungry.

Old abandoned ocean is shortcut to Krispy Kreme in Riverhead, off exit sixty-something.

"You wanna get all plain or something different?"

Eelio long, slimy, yellow and looks like snake.

"Cream ones," says Arn.

Eelio makes jacking off motion with fin.

"What that supposed to mean?"

"Where the cream comes from."

Arn smells cat.

Wrinkles up snout.

Rusty hook breaks surface.

Tied to crappy tuna line.

Arn catches with mouth and snaps.

Arn and Eelio swim to surface.

See small boat.

Furry Cantag sits in boat with fishing stick and snapped line.

"Get new hook, Cantag!" laughs Arn.

"You're a hooligan, Sharcarnahan!" Cantag shakes paw over his head.

"This is our ocean," says Eelio.

"Tuna house rules," says Cantag. "Everything between the shore and rig is mine. I sprayed this place, I own this ocean. I own you."

"That's where he stashes tuna," says Eelio.

"Hey, maybe we go to oil rig and grab free snack," says Arn.

"Don't mess with me," says Cantag. "I'm a nice cat but not when some hooligans step all over my turf."

"Forget you," says Eelio and swims away.

Arn follows.

"We should get free snack," says Arn.

"You heard what Cantag said," says Eelio.

"So?"

"Who knows what kind of equipment he has on that rig?"

Arn shrugs fins.

"I swear," says Eelio, "One day that cat's gonna go Chief Brody on you."

"Don't be pussy," says Arn.

"That'll be the day." Eelio rolls his eyes.

"What you mean by that?" says Arn.

"Nothing man, nothing."

"Whatever." Arn swims ahead of Eelio in direction of rig.

"C'mon," says Eelio from behind.

Big storm turned rig over on its side.

Arn picks up scent of oil.

Big flat piece of metal and girders stick up out of water, only parts you can see from surface.

Here Cantag sleep sometimes and somewhere he hides stash of nice fish to eat.

Even from mile, Arn picks up scent of Cantag's spray.

Smells sweet to Arn.

He wonders what it taste like.

Butterscotch drop.

Arn looks up at platform through water.

Sees blurry blonde girl with curly hair.

Sits on platform and beams of light float around her.

Arn breaks surface.

No beams.

Girl dressed in white teddy.

She sits on knees with arms pulled back behind her.

"Who are you?" Eelio splashes fins around in water.

Girl looks drugged off pills, green eyes float back and forth.

She not say anything.

"Who are you?" says Arn in soothing tone. "Tell me."

"Help me," girl says.

Water bubbles float up all around Arn.

Eelio slides close.

Arn feels shiver run through eel's long body.

Sees round shadow below.

Knife shoots through water followed by red hand.

Arn moves between blade and Eelio just in time to catch inside himself.

"Get out of here!" man with knife screams and draws out word here so it sounds like siren and his face is red and angry like his hands.

His blonde crew cut flares out.

Fat girl dressed in purple jumpsuit and built like Teletubbie pops out of water behind Arn and scratches on his fin.

"Jerikant!" she says.

"Serikant, my daughter!"

"Yall has no business here," says Jerikant and Arn is sure this is his name because word is written in gold letters down sleeves of yellow spandex jumpsuit.

"Arn, c'mon," Eelio splashes around like crazy.

Arn wants to swim away but freezes at look in Jerikant and Serikant's eyes.

Look of meanness so horrible it makes him feel empty inside.

And sick.

Girl has wavy brown hair.

Baby Arn watches from under water and it makes rest of her curly too. Curly and unreal.

The less real she can be to Baby Arn the better.

"Bite now," says B.T. Sharcarnahan.

Baby Arn's father never liked him, always thinks he is gay or weak.

Girl on long yellow rubber boat shaped like dildo.

She on back.

Seven people sit in front of her.

She holds on to smaller girl with same brown curly hair. Baby Arn glad he not have to bite something small as that.

B.T. picks one on back for him.

"B.T. tell you once and not again. Bite girl now!"

Baby Arn swims up slowly behind boat and hears screams of people on shore who watch his head break water.

Girl with brown hair screams loud as Baby Arn closes teeth around girl's legs and pulls girl off back of boat.

Girl lets go of other girl who screams, "Mommy, mommy!" as Baby Arn pulls her under the water.

Girl doesn't move and Baby Arn can't stand taste of her so he lets her go and girl floats up dead to surface.

Water fills with blood and yellow boat deflates.

People all swim to shore and little girl is alone without mommy.

"Bite more!" says B.T.

"No," says Baby Arn, "won't bite more."

"Are you some kind of faggot?" says B.T.

"Leave me alone," says Baby Arn. "I no like to bite people, I no like to bite anything."

"You're disgusting," says B.T.

He snaps out jaws and bites Baby Arn's head and eyes so Baby Arn can't see or hear anymore and his head is full of agony.

Blood pours out of Baby Arn's head and he floats up towards

the sun.
Baby Arn flips over on back.
Floats.
And bleeds.

Arn not stop until sure him and Eelio far enough from rig.

Eelio out of breath.

Not make sense when he talk.

"Chill," says Arn and puts fin around Eelio.

"What are we gonna do?" says Eelio.

"We do nothing," says Arn. "We go to Krispy Kreme and eat donuts."

"That girl—"

"That girl some slut, probably have threesome with father and daughter monsters."

"She said Help me," says Eelio.

Arn feels chill remembering Jerikant.

Water still all around him.

Normal.

"Pay attention," says Eelio. "She said Help me," and then Eelio mouths the words "Help me!"

"Help meeeeeeeeeeee!"

Red hand clutches Eelio's head and sweeps him out of water and across knife blade in quick motion like shucking oyster.

Then rest of Jerikant rises up out of water.

Salt water drips off cracked smile as he drops Eelio's body into ocean.

Eelio looks like yellow and red streamers on handlebars of girl's bike if made of flesh.

"Help who?" says Jerikant. "Help who?"

"Why you doing this?" says Arn.

"God gave man dominion over animals," Jerikant shrieks

help me, i'm hungry / **129**

and Arn wishes he has ears and hands to cover them with.

Arn feels Jerikant's knife blade sink into belly.

Jerikant pumps and pumps knife, turns Arn's guts to juice.

Arn twists head around to get mouth near Jerikant's neck.

Jerikant reaches around Arn with free hands to pull Arn closer.

Arn uses space between to open mouth.

Jerikant screams as Arn closes jaws around neck and chews right through.

Arn swallows Jerikant's fat red head whole and even with own guts streaming out behind, points snout in direction of oil rig.

Saving girl was last thing Eelio ever wanted to do.

Baby Arn floats up to surface.
Pieces of yellow rubber fan out around him.
Baby Arn can feel heat of sun closer to the surface.
B.T. was father but he not care. He killed Baby Arn for being pussy.
"Hey man," says baby voice.
Arn tries to see who it is, it is dark though and blurry. Something long and yellow.
"Hey dad, we have to help him," says voice again.
Lots of long and yellow things surround Arn.
"Don't worry," says voice. "My name's Baby Eelio, you're not alone, I'm going to help you."
Eels all grab Arn with teeth and pull him back down into water.
One shoves rotten fish into his mouth.

Serikant naked, out of Teletubbie suit now.

In each hand a large machete.

Stands over blonde girl and watches each drop of pussy juice fall into girl's whimpering mouth.

Arn sees shiny spots floating in water and old head scar hurts bad.

It is hard for Arn to get energy to talk.

Jerikant shank him bad.

He is dying worse than time B.T. bite his head.

Serikant crouched down onto girl, pressing pussy against her.

"Ah'ma get yall good," she says.

"Serikant," says Arn.

Serikant shrieks and rocks back and forth on top of girl.

"Jerikant help us! Jerikant help us!"

"Jerikant not help you," says Arn, "Jerikant dead!"

Arn pushes snout out of water and Serikant jump off girl.

"Ah'm not goin in after yall," says Serikant.

"I get you then," says Arn.

He tries to bite but she swings blade so much faster than Jerikant.

Searing pain shoots through back and dorsal fin slides off and floats next to him.

"You've lost all rights to your life," says Serikant.

"Please stop now," says Arn.

Serikant only laughs.

"Let girl go please."

Arn floats on his side with dorsal fin just a streaming red slit.

He can barely see Serikant.

He can barely feel water around him.

"Ouch yall."

He hears Serikant scream now.

Arn sees Serikant clutch at something shiny hooked into pussy lip.

She shrieks in agony as she is yanked off platform. She splashes into water.

Arn feels like he not alone, like he is warm, so he closes his black eyes.

"I don't like people messing about on my rig," says Cantag the fishercat.

Boat floats over to dead shark.

"I took your advice and got a new hook, the kind that goes both ways."

Shakes his paw at Serikant, who is struggling to keep head above water.

"Looks like I caught me a whale," he says.

TAKE TWO

willie smith

You enter the den. Take off your hat. Occupy the couch. Need to take the mind off the troubles. Turn on the tv.

Two guys in a Chevy take off into the black-and-white night. They just took off a convenience at gunpoint.

The one guy does a Bogart takeoff. Lights a butt. Growls out the side of his trap, "What's the take?"

Not taking his eyes off the road, the other snaps, "How would I know? We count it when we get there."

"Take it," the Bogart purrs, "easy. Just fishing for a ballpark."

The other takes a hand off the wheel. Snaps on the radio.

"Wet, cold and delicious…," the dashboard speaker boasts. "National beer!"

"Think we took over a thou?" The Bogart sneers, leaks smoke, a passing streetlight catching the tips of his incisors. "I say it ain't worth it, anything under a thou."

The dash bursts into song: "And while I'm at it I'm proud to say – it's brewed on the shores of the Chesapeake Bay!"

"Look – I gotta concentrate on the driving. Find some music wouldja?"

"This is music," the Bogart mutters to the windshield, as the Impala flies down a ramp onto the Interstate. "These people are harmonizing about suds. I like songs like this."

You consider taking a pee. Then think why not wait a sec. Let a bit more urine accumulate; bladder swell to optimum volume to void; not yet painful but precisely the act to perform.

"These people are jingling for money. This is a *commercial*."

"You want," the Bogie kills the radio, "*feeling*?" Clears throat. Taps a foot in four-four on the floorboard. Takes off Sinatra: "I'm from Milwaukee and I oughta know – it's Blatz beer, Blatz beer, wherever you go!"

"For Christ's sake shut up!"

"Smoother, fresher, less filling that's clear…!"

Your wife hails from Milwaukee. Suburb just outside. Your wife who just took off with Bud Miller – kid down the block, clerk at the local convenience. Makes all of six bucks an hour. Now making your wife's lovely white body buck on the bed in some cheap hotel room.

"Blatz is Milwaukee's fi-i-nest beer!"

The Impala lopes off the Interstate. Winds down a two-lane unimproved. Hacks a right. Charges up a dirt road into the trees. The set looks too bright for moonlight; but no harder to swallow than the two-bit acting.

You wonder if you should get up. Visit the kitchen. Crack a Pabst. Take a gulp. The act of swallowing stimulates the urge to urinate. A medical fact that, when you think about it, makes sense.

Then amble down the hall into the can. By the time you stand over the bowl, be the perfect moment to commence.

They reach the hideout. A shadowy unpainted one-room shack choked with ivy and maybe that's supposed to be Spanish moss.

Wipe to thugs inside hideout.

The impersonator stumbles around, while the other strikes a kitchen match off an empty apple crate; gets a lamp lit.

In the kerosene glow each locates a crate – a stack leans against one wall, half-a-dozen others tumbled here and there. Each drags his crate to the center of the room.

They squat on the low boxes, knees up in their faces. The driver pulls the wad from a pocket of his gray pullover.

They settle down to the business of counting – sorting bills into piles according to denomination, laying out the piles on an upended third crate.

Solemn music builds – a brewski jingle in a minor key. The self-conscious imitator – dressed in a Salvation Army black suit jacket and open collar button-down white shirt – leans over, counting twenties, tens, fives, while the other concentrates on the tall pile of wrinkled singles.

The movie seems to be morphing from film noir into low-budget horror. You expect a gust to blow out the flame, a wolf to howl, a chick to shriek or a zombie to materialize out of the shadows.

And there you are – thinking monochrome as the characters you approach.

Spotting yourself in a movie a total shock. For one, it isn't your mirror image – the face you ordinarily recognize. You are moreover so small, stiff, slow. Especially when playing a reanimated corpse creeping up on two losers about to join you in death.

You take off Karloff – Frankenstein just another zombie with a bolt, bad stitches, big shoes. The monster, that is. You know nothing about acting. (You fit right in). But you do know Frankenstein is the creator's name – not the monster's.

You still vaguely need to pee. Although the urge is dying, fading like a ghost in the dawn. Too busy concentrating on the part?

Whatever, you need to make this believable – believable as the holes the wife shot in your head before taking off with Bud Miller. You still fail to understand why she took such violence into her own head. You a twenty-nine year old city planner with a brilliant future; not quite yet a beerbelly; career just about to take off.

Bogie peers up from counting the take. Mimes you gawking into the wife's automatic...

Smiling she counts to almost five before squeezing all the way the trigger. She likely not knowing at what number she'll fire. She – unlike you – no planner; teaches modern dance part time; from the start a marriage made in limbo...

The driver, too scared to scream, wets himself.

With both hands you take off Bogie's head. Clomp next over to the other, who sits frozen in his own waste. The chaos on his face makes it almost worth it.

SNORT

daniel allen cox

Our favorite hangout was comatose as usual, the way we liked it. I satat the bar with Lewis, staring at the tropical wallpaper covered in graffiti, at swastikas and palm trees, peeling the label off my beer bottle. Lewis ignored me and stared at the television.

A whiff of his skunky aftershave made me turn to him and count the tattoos that crawled up his neck, past little hairs that were stuck in a permanent bristle.

"Hey freak of nature, I hate you."

He wasn't listening.

Lewis wasn't the ugliest skinhead in town. His nose, as far as I could tell, had never been broken.

There were no shots of tabasco and tequila in front of him, no cocaine cradled in his palms ready to be hoovered up his nose when the bartender played the songs we liked, no bandages lying around to absorb my blood when he wanted to play rough. He was watching golf and drinking mimosas, trying his damnedest to make me feel like I didn't exist. He was acting differently and I knew why.

"That's enough," I said, "you're making me sick."

He pointed to the nearly invisible white ball lost in the TV sky.

"Swallowing that ball through your ear would make you sick, too."

"Maybe I would like that."

It was the sort of talk I wanted, but hardly enough to keep me happy. Whose time did he think he was wasting?

I twisted his ear with a pair of needle-nose pliers I kept for situations like this, clamping the tool down on his gristle, hoping it would transform him into the Lewis I needed to help me unwind pleasantly into the weekend.

He turned to me, shaking, and I could see the crashing surf of violence frothing in his eyes, about to overflow and make him punish my body. He snorted and his nose-ring trembled in the television light. But the real Lewis was still sleeping within this docile version of him. He just put a hand on my shoulder and let a smile slowly infect his face.

"Let's play pool," he said calmly, blotting his bloody ear with the shoulder of his cut-off t-shirt.

I knew that a better way to get to him was to root through some fresh wounds.

"I can understand if you couldn't help yourself. She was the bomb and you're nothing but an animal that's learned to mimic a few human words."

A swollen vein danced on his forehead, slow and pulsing.

"Did she remind you of your mom, the Viagra whore?"

He crushed a cube of pool chalk in his hand and let the blue dust rain down on his Doc Martens. It was difficult for him to ignore my insults. But he managed to turn away from me.

I knew I was losing. I chalked my cue as if I were sharpening it, ready for another go at him.

"Tell me you hurt her. Tell me you eight-balled her before you snuffed her out."

No response. He broke cleanly and the balls ricocheted around without falling into any of the pockets.

"Was it easy for her to scream with her pretty throat slit open?"

"Your shot," he said.

"No, it's your turn."

"I missed."

I slapped a hundred on the edge of the pool table.

"It's still your turn."

Fresh from a bank machine, I wouldn't have to play for hours.

It had given me a blood rush to see his brutish, unshaven mug in the paper that morning, all jaw and hulking deltoids. The world was starting to hear about my Lewis. It made me jealous as hell.

A legal technicality had set him free, but I knew that he'd gotten off because of his charm. Because he was Lewis. And now he was acting like he knew I wasn't the only one with a mortal crush on him.

He knocked the white ball clear onto the floor. I slipped another hundred into the back pocket of his jeans and felt up the crack of his ass.

He was happy to keep playing. I was furious, lividly crushing imaginary skulls in my fists. It was time to push this timid bruiser over the edge, beyond the point of holding back. I craved a pure, undiluted pummeling that would give me broken teeth to swallow and some creeping bruises to decorate me blue and mottled brown. I made it easy for him. I jabbed my pool cue into his nuts. He bent over, reaching up to fondle my nose, as if feeling the bone he needed to bust off my face.

"Stop being a pussy and give what's coming to me."

I closed my eyes and waited for the ecstasy to hit.

But as he unfolded from his pain-absorbing hunch he just flicked my nose and laughed. He tickled my chin with the cocktail parasol from his mimosa and stared into my eyes. I was losing my mind. Did killing somebody really give one such internal peace?

He leaned over and breathed into my ear, holding back a whisper.

"Please," I mouthed, melting into his chest.

"Only if I can kill you, too."

Lewis kissed me deeply and drew a line across my throat

with his thumb. I gave him the rest of my money.

A MAN IN BLUE
steve finbow

A car pulls up close to the house, it must have driven off the road through the field, across the grass; he could not hear the stones pop and spit on the graveled road. There is no dramatic exhalation of birds from branches. No dog barking. No warning. They are just there at the door. Close. Closer still. He can hear them outside. Hear their heavy boots, their coarse and booming voices. Their noise cuts through the trees. Their sound leeches into the silence he has built around himself. E's in ere, he can hear. Ow d'you fuckin' know? I fuckin' know. I just fuckin' do. Don't touch the lil cun' til I've 'ad a go. Righ'? He hears. Righ'. He is unsure whether to stand and face them. Stand in the door ready for when they come through. Inevitably. Or huddle in the corner, prone, useless. He could hide elsewhere in the house. He knows it well. Maybe he should get out. The back door. But there would be someone there waiting. Inevitably. Would they find him? Inevitably. He backs into the corner, hugs his knees in his arms, puts his chin between them and peers out at the door, looking up through his fringe. The house surrounds him in its practicality, it was made for this, to harbour, to comfort, to enclose. Nothing from without within. You go round back. You come wiv me. And keep it down, he can hear them say. A man says, Shu' i'.. Another man says, Shu' i'. There are fifteen feet between him and the front door and within that space, a chair, a two-seater sofa, a low pine table, and a rug bunched at the far right corner, its edge, tucked under, makes it look like an eyelid. It winks, blinks. Across the window, patterned curtains are drawn. On the right wall is a painting, he cannot remember if it is a landscape, or if it isn't. The lights are out. He has become used to the room unilluminated. He's become used to it. Shu' the fuck up, he hears. Listen. Ssh! There is quiet. Quiet and dark. He blinks and waits. His heart thumps. He stands. He raises his hands above his head, grasps his hands together, interlocks his fingers, and the cartilages crack in unison. Dyou 'ear tha'? Wha'? Tha' noise. Like cracking. Nah. Well, I fuckin' well 'eard sumfing. A man says, Let's do the door. He edges toward the stairs and takes them two at a time not worrying about the noise the wood makes as it gives under the cheap foam-backed carpet. There are three doors – a toilet/bathroom, two bedrooms – and a storage cupboard. The voices sound far away, paper on a bonfire, children on a school bus. He sits with his back to the bathroom door. He hears them push against the door. Hears their straining. Isn't what they'll do to him that he fears, it is what he will not do to protect himself, or what he will do. That's it. That's more like it. Downstairs now. Put your ear to the door and listen to the men. Come on, give it some. I am. Shu' i', youse two. Try the window. They whisper unsuccessfully. Go roun' the back in case the lil fucker does a runner, a man says. If we looked through the keyhole, we'd see two men. One dressed in an expensive suit twiddling his cufflinks, rubbing his nose with his right index finger. He takes a break to straighten his tie and move his head in a circular movement to relax his neck muscles and, as he does this, his chin makes a mini-orbit within the central movement, more pronounced, more gestural. His hair is greased back, fifties, gelified. The other man is squatter, more rigid; he wears jeans and a T-shirt, work boots. Two others are trying the windows around the back. Let's just do it, T-shirt man says. 'Old your fuckin' 'orses, the other says. Let's do i' righ'. No fuck ups. Ready? Upstairs. He's gone. Where could he be? The front door splinters. Not a word is spoken. The lights go on. A man says, check the kitchen, I'll check upstairs. Where's those other two wankers? We're 'ere, he hears them say. He feels their weight and heft beneath him, the pulsing momentum of their quest slowly subsiding, breathing easy, cooling down, as if a beast resting after a chase, licking its paws, licking its bloody maw, its tongue reeking, its eyes refulgent, slumped in the entrance hall. He can feel his scalp crawl. He wants to vomit. He doesn't.

SAMARITAN'S FLIGHT

suzanne nielsen

Teresa pulled back the torn denim that covered her stucco white legs to reveal two bleeding pedestals. One of her shoes had lost its way in flight, just like Samaritan, or Sam, for short. She started cursing; why would a hospital leave her alone with 33 patients? Why didn't she run faster? Why did Skynard ever write *Free Bird*? And that damned dog, everyone knows a dog's howl is the setting for doom.

Rushing water and discombobulated thoughts swarmed inside her inebriated brain. Moments ago she was escorting the psych patients outdoors for a game of volleyball. Then she was climbing the cement wall chasing Sam, who had decided to fly, then run. Now she was staring at Gem Lake on an early March evening in Minnesota. A dog howled from the other side of the lake. From the hospital building up on the hill, a group of medical professionals were hurrying their way down to the water to descend upon her, ask her questions and bring her back inside to finish off an activity with the remaining 32 patients.

Teresa attempted to go in after him, got up to her waist in the icy water and knew it would pull her under as well. So she watched from shore. Teresa watched Sam's head make its way out into the dark water. She threatened him first:

"Sam, you're not going to pull this off, three days in pj's, no smokes..." But Sam kept his destination intact, his voice carrying over the open water as though through a megaphone.

"I must be traveling on, now, 'cause there's too many places I've got to see."

The dog in the distance continued to howl in tune with Sam's strokes and in defiance of Teresa's attempts to draw him back.

"Sam, smokes on me for a week, your favorite, Virginia Slims…" she shouted over the water. Sam was slowing in motion, but his legs were still treading underneath as his head kept bobbing while he sang in a sweet, struggling voice.

"Please don't take it so badly, 'cause Lord knows I'm to blame."

Sam was tiring. Teresa was pulling at her hair, pacing back and forth on shore.

"Things just couldn't be the same. Cause I'm as free as a bird now, and this bird…" And with that he went down.

He came up briefly, but only to go back down again, quietly, as Teresa was bombarded by the staff, asking her what had happened, telling her she did the right thing by not attempting to save him.

"The water's too frigid," said Dr. Strom.

"Teresa, let's go back to the building and get some dry clothes on you and write up this accident report," said nurse Montegue.

"You can't save the world, Teresa, some you'll never change," Montegue continued.

Teresa made her way up the hill with Montegue. One shoe on, one lost in flight. Had the howling dog lost his innocence, now silenced across the water? Teresa wondered.

3.8 SECONDS

matt maxwell

Gangly Martez, four days shy of twelve, rocked on the mound, stepping back at an angle, swinging his arms around his waist to meet behind, brought his right arm up in a swooping arc, kept his left arm dangling like a limp, dead weight, strode long as if over a puddle, picked the ball from his ear and whisked it home, trailing his right leg, dragging his toes across the loose dirt.

Spindly Frank, having already been painfully plunked by three errant pitches, timid and not determined, his eyes increasingly like cartoonish balloons, stopped breathing, gripped the bat, trying to squeeze the leather-wrapped aluminum for a magical elixir, slid his back foot away from the catcher, and began to create distance between himself and the plate.

Chunky Kevin, knees tired from the pressure of the oppressive humidity, saw the ball rifling for a strike, clinched his fist behind his back in anticipation of the thumping arrival or possible deflected blow that would ricochet off his poorly-fitted equipment, shifted his glove to the arrival station, and squeezed his brown eyes shut inside shells of fat.

Stellar Defense, when compared to the rest of the league, eyes on their erratic pitcher, some chanting mantras to confuse the batter, some knowing the ball would avoid them like it had all game and the game before, the shortstop on his toes, creeping in for fear his dad would see him stand flat-footed like the third baseman and yell at him, the left fielder stumbling quietly over a clump of grass in the pock-marked and dangerous outfield, tensed and thought about who to throw the ball to under the present circumstance.

Disheartened Coach Angermeier, standing near third base, trying to watch Frank with one eye while the other perused the seventeen year old girl flaunting in front of the concession stand, hopefully to buy a Lik-N-Stix, had forgotten just how many outs his team had, knowing that Frank's doomed inevitability would add another to the total, wondered if any beer was left in the concession stand fridge, not that his pony keg belly needed any more.

Spastic Suzanne, three years old, speaking with a heavy lisp but shrieking in an abnormally high frequency, ran around the small wooden pirate ship beyond the outfield fence, her unshod feet light brown from the dirt, screaming when Chase or Alex or Nick or John, all boys slightly older, ran near her while they played tag, but chasing, her short legs barely bending, the boy who was it.

Unforgiving Sun, a nuclear anvil pressing on the field, a baneful bulb burning the grass, the players, the fans, a force field pushing away cloud cover, rained malevolent heat.

Tense Keith, glaring at the field, seeing the entire diamond, noting that Sam, the right fielder, had never moved into position, never even taken his glove from his hip, and compiled it in the case files as an argument against why his son, who wore a $145 Rawlings Heart of the Hide glove, played only when the score was out of hand.

Nervous Christie, trying to read a Grisham novel during the sporadic cheering and yelling and senseless conversations of the surrounding parents, pondered her ex-husband's potential mood after not only being banned from the field for obscene, violent, drunken behavior over a call against their son but recently being served a restraining order by her and her boyfriend of two years (who passively watched the game beside her), knew that sooner of later he would make an appearance that would entail police presence again, hoping that Joey, simple, cheerful Joey, would be absent.

Tumbling Rawlings baseball, made to manufacturer specifics, pearly leather and red skull n' bones stitching the conveyor of dreams, visions, hopes, and nightmares, an orb of glory for one, a ball of scars for another, whistled gently, for the fast pitch really wasn't that fast and didn't attain the fearsome whine of cannon-armed Drew, a missile for a target, honing in with inaccurate precision.

Doubtful Thomas, father of league-famed Douglas, a man possessing only rudimentary baseball knowledge, learning the infield fly rule and then forgetting it two days later, refuses to understand why a left-hander cannot play second or short or third, who writes continuously, praying for one small break, pondered the idea of remixing a previously published story, much like bands remake another group's song and gain notoriety, why can't he remix a story, say, "The Cask of Amontillado," put his personal spin on it, and release it?

Hussy Susan, playing with her ankle chain, revolving it around her olive-tanned skin, attracted looks that started at her four-inch stilettos, roamed up her bared calves, to her tourniquet camel toe Capris, to her adorned belly button, prominent chest, obviously fake they were so high and round and concrete, to her frightening face and hair, a mirror of an evil clown beset by blood lips and crayon-streaked cheeks, hair a wild configuration of electromagnetics and a pudding bowl.

Cocksure Umpire, noting the batter who would rather hit off his Playstation, the angle of the incoming rotational orb, strobes of red flashing on a canvas of marble white, breathed deeply through his inherited humped nose, distantly remembering the parent of the batting team who least week threatened him for missing a call, prepared to call a strike, shifting his weight prematurely.

Inebriated Jerry, hat pulled low on his brow, obscuring the sun and his eyes, a Big Gulp in his trembling left hand, half full of warm Budweiser, eyed his enemy Randy's nape, so vulnerable, so blind to the kids running behind him to and from the concession stand, the parents chatting about the defective lights, the impatient competitors waiting for the next game, the 9mm pointed at his skull as he held Christie's unringed hand, the tan line non-existent.

Spindly Frank, eyes closed, brought the bat around in a helicopter sweeping arc, wild, rotational, a wave intended merely to please Coach Angermeier, who watched the curvaceous teen bend over to pick up dropped change, heard the gun blast and jumped and released the bat which connected solidly with the sideways rotating Rawlings, that spun neatly past the petrified Martez, between the terrified second and first basemen and rolled harmlessly into the outfield where the lackadaisical fielder finally dropped his glove, only this time to his feet, and Kevin, through the iron bars of his mask, so much representing prison, watched the wave of adults part, opening his view to the wooden pirate ship where Suzanne had finally stopped screaming, and Keith fell to the side, striking his knuckles on a trash can, and Thomas, whose daydreaming ended abruptly, urinated in an eruption, something Susan might have noticed had she not fallen when a heel stuck in the cracks of the wobbly planks of the bleachers, and landed on her nose near a mound of peanut shells, only slightly larger than the dust mound the umpire created when he fell in a protective ball, breathless, to the ground, landing with a quieter thump than did Christie's boyfriend of two years when his corpse fell from the bleachers, under the sun unwinking, unyielding.

IN DENA

ken ryan

1

The moon is red, the clouds black, the effect like blood in water. I drive the Lincoln like a bastard, heading right for it.

3

I light a cigarette while crossing two lanes at once and I make exit seventeen. I nearly take a Fiat with me. Smoking's dangerous. I shake the match and toss it out the window.

5

It's late and the parking lot's mine; I take the spot by the door. The ashtray is full of crushed butts. I open the car door and empty it onto the white line.

The lights are on inside. I see you framed in neon, like a prophet in stained glass. You're reading. You know I'm coming.

I go in. I say, Dena, and the brass bell rattles. I salivate.

You snap the spine of the book and lay it like a dead bird on the cash register. You don't look at me. Then, you do. I'm thirsty. You're coy.

I need something.

I know.

I'm serious.

I know.

You quit the stool and come around the counter. There's a pickle barrel of shaved ice and corked bottlenecks. You take one and pull it out and waggle it and the ice water sluices down your wrist.

Cabernet's on sale.

You're joking.

Not good enough for you?

Get serious.

You turn the bottle and push it head first through the ice. I'm running out of time. I need another smoke. I light one and you don't say a word.

You walk down the rye and whiskey aisle and I grab a nip of something from the basket on the counter and crack the top. Your poison is in my mouth. You turn.

Fleischman's?

Why not Wild Irish Rose? I pocket the empty nip. You trying to kill me?

Hmm.

You keep walking. You drag a finger along the bottles as you go. I take another nip; it goes into my pocket.

Rum?

Maybe.

I join you at the intersection of Johnnie Walker and Captain Morgan. He's a wicked pirate; he dares me from the label. He's calling me a pussy.

No. No rum. I turn the bottle around, make him kiss his twin. Who's the pussy now?

There's always beer. You wave at the chest like one of Bob Barker's androids.

Takes too long, Dena. And I'll be in the pisser all night.

You've had it. I've had it. You say, you got money tonight? You toss your head to your shoulder as if someone's pulled on your ear.

Tonight, yeah.

Let me see it.

I take fifty from my shirt pocket and drop the cigarette, the fifty that Jonsey owed me.

You snatch it and it's in your fist, gone. I step on the butt.

What do you want?
I want out.
You want out?
Just give it to me.

You nod. You get it. You touch your finger to your lip and the bills are still in your fist, somewhere. You bend down to the bottom shelf and now there's two things I want. You come up with a bottle, a genie's bottle.

What is it?
Courvoisier.
Is it good?
It's VSOP.
Is it good?
Yeah.
I want to try it.
We're still open.
Close.

You do the right thing. You toss my cash on the counter and take a key ring from a hook and lock the door. You turn off the lights. You're a spook in the neon backlight. You take a jackknife out of your hip pocket and give it to me. I cut the seal and pull the cork and drink. It's not bad.

Is that what you want?
I drink again.
It's not in my head.
What?
The booze, it's not in my head.
What do you want?
I want out.
I drink more.

You take the bottle from me. You fill your mouth.

7

We're in the back room. You're holding my bottle and I'm

pushing cases of booze, stacking them. You tell me where to put them. I make a square brown throne. I make another. Jim Beam for me and Jack Daniel's for you.

The boxes were heavy. Give me my bottle.

Sit down.

I do. It's a good seat but my hands hang over the boxes like a faggot's. I don't care; I'm tired. You sit next to me. You pour poison into my mouth; my chin and throat are wet. It's not in my head.

Good?

It's not in my head.

It's my best stuff.

It's not enough.

You set the bottle on your armrest, on the case of Jack.

11

You stand over me. My legs are between yours. I'm looking at the ceiling. You're holding my hand, squeezing my arm. You run your nail from the inside of my elbow to my wrist. I can't feel it; I don't care. You kiss the course you made in me. One kiss, elbow to wrist.

You're in my head. You're there.

Your mouth is fucked up with blood. You take my other hand and it's the same kiss, long. I hear the jackknife hit the floor.

13

What's it like?

It's like nothing.

Is it good enough?

Yeah. It's about right.

There's nothing in me, nothing but Dena in my head. And I'm in Dena.

HOW I QUIT TORTURING POODLES

delphine lecompte

I've spent the past three months putting money on crippled horses, thankfully it wasn't my dough, but i feel broke and gutted nevertheless; it was a nefarious welsh carpenter who crippled them, i saw him steal into the stables with his phallic welsh sledge-hammer, he was wearing cheap khaki boots, blue jeans, a faded blur t-shirt, a fake tan, a murderous gleam on his chin and a conspicuous stetson hat, i tried to stop him, but before i could reach him an ill-tempered shetland pony broke my collarbone with its shit-caked fetlock, it also bit the cluster of aardvark-shaped warts off my nape, and the hyena-shaped melanoma off my left buttock, and then it lashed me with its mane, and with its saddle flap, i eventually passed out, i woke up after seventy fixed races, that's why i quit gambling: it got too predictable, so now i'm resuming being bored, today i'm bored on the dewy threshold of a disused nuclear fallout shelter, i'm so bored i could torture the pinkish poodle that's creeping by, it's too late now, it crossed the street, christopher the illiterate rentboy is coming towards me, i'm so bored i could snap his delectable elbows, "how are you?" asks he in his contrived choir boy squeak, i shrug, he sits himself next to me, we watch a vulgar village pageant pass, three hags dressed up as harlots pelt us with cloves of garlic, we watch a miserable skinny asian boy throw himself in front of a huge yellow truck that's transporting albanian garden gnomes, we watch a hirsute geezer pump his puny chest, we watch another hirsute geezer put a blanket over the not so serene ashen face, we watch the ambulance drive away, we watch the relentless sun sink, and then the pinkish poodle reappears, "that's fifica!" christopher joyfully exclaims, "it's got a penis", "so?", "isn't fifica a girl's name?", "i don't know", "let's torture fifica", "why?", "do we need a reason to put our boots into a filthy pinkish poodle?" christopher contemplates the torturing of fifica, meanwhile the poodle is licking dried-up raspberry jam off my right shin, "ok, let's do it" the ill rentboy belches after fourteen minutes of tiresome contemplating, "which part shall we torture first?" i ask him, he looks bemused and resumes contemplating, meanwhile fifica is licking congealed blood off my left thumb, "its belly?" christopher suggests, "no, not its belly, thick cunt" i snarl, the illiterate rentboy starts to sulk, we watch a few stars shoot, we watch a wino choke on a peanut butter sandwich, we watch a surly raven-haired nymphette trip over a stuffed one-eyed deer and fall flat on her face, we watch a guy who looks like tom selleck snog a nondescript slapper, we watch a chubby black boy spraypaint 'blains upon thy oxen' on the windscreen of a smug grey audi, "its front paws?" christopher gloomily mumbles, "no, not its front paws, daft twat" i impatiently hiss, we watch a ruddy flemish postman chuck ten letters in a wishing well, we watch the sun come up, i half-heartedly put my left boot into fifica's sickly chest, the poodle shows its dull yellow teeth, and its hopelessly swollen gums, and its strangely spotted palate, we watch fifica retreat whilst keeping an eye on me, we watch the poodle coming back, "its tail?" i roll my eyes, get up and run away from the ill rentboy and the poodle with the strange name.

CONTRIBUTORS' NOTES

Apart from running the UK's only moose sanctuary, **DEAN BAKER** has been published in Wild Child, New Camp Horror, Thieves Jargon, Skive, Zygote in My Coffee, Gonzobeats, and Blue Almonds magazines. He writes feverishly, travels extensively and currently maintains a healthy sense of humour and a sunny disposition in his native Middlesex.

BOZ BOWLES lives, teaches, and writes in Greenville, SC. He holds an M.F.A. from Virginia Commonwealth University where he was on the editorial staff of Blackbird: an on-line journal of literature and the arts. His work has appeared or is forthcoming in several literary journals and magazines, including Red Rock Review, River Oak Review, Dream Network Journal, Art Times Journal, and Rainbow Curve. In the past, he has been a blues drummer, a dump truck driver, a shovel kicker, and a burger flipper.

For **MIKE BOYLE**, there's been street life, bar life and factory life in several cities. There have been songs with several bands, poems, stories, home recordings and several novel messes. Currently a factory slug that runs printing presses in Harrisburg, PA.

DANIEL ALLEN COX is the author of the story collection Episodes of Deflated Magic (Fever Press, 2004), and the novella Tattoo This Madness In (Dusty Owl Press, 2006). He is the Artist Spotlight Editor of Outsider Ink magazine and has written interviews for the seminal punk newspaper New York Waste.

MARVIN DORSEY owns and manages a construction company as well as commercial/industrial properties. He was born and raised in south Louisiana: oil fields, sugar cane, big lakes and marshes. With all its primitive charms, he emotionally survived by looking through literary windows into a larger world: Tom Whalen, T. Walter Herbert, Italo Calvino, Updike, Welty, etc. He and his wife have three children. They're well.

MALON EDWARDS is a fiction writer currently living on the North Side of Chicago.

P. S. EHRLICH is the author-in-progress of 13 BLACK CATS UNDER A LADDER, of which Never Tell Your Birthday Wish is an excerpt. Others can be found at his website, www.skeeterkitefly.com.

STEVE FINBOW is a Londoner. He has worked for the artist Richard Long, the biographer Victor Bockris, and was researcher/editor for the poet Allen Ginsberg. He is Associate Fiction Editor of The Absinthe Literary Review and Contributing Editor for Me Three. He is also a writer with Quarantine Theatre Company. His book Pond Scum and Other Effluvia is available here: http://www.pulpbits.com.

JAMES GRECO does not exist.

JAMES GRINWIS lives in MA. His work has appeared in Conjunctions, American Poetry Review, Gettysburg Review, and many others. An E-chapbook of his flash fiction can be found at Pulpbits Press.

BRADLEY MASON HAMLIN lives in Sacramento, California. His poetry, short stories, and articles have appeared in several small press books, magazines, and literary journals in print and on line. Brad & his wife Nicky own Mystery Island Publications and publish an ongoing in-print literary pop culture magazine called: Mystery Island Magazine. Recent work includes the publication of Tough Company by singer/songwriter Tom Russell, featuring: Charles Bukowski. Brad is also the creator of the metaphysical crime series: the Secret Society, featuring the Intoxicated Detective. For more information about Hamlin and other wild things—visit: www.mysteryisland.net.

ANDY HENION writes because his professional football career fizzled early, in eighth grade. He likes his beer loud, his music dark and his costars droll. His fiction has appeared in a few dozen print and online journals, not including The New Yorker, The Atlantic, Harper's and Playboy. He was born the day before Armstrong planted his flag on the moon. He's of average length.

ERIC JONES is a charlatan. His codswallop has appeared in such odious hardscrabble publications as Or-else, LOAF, La Pensee Savage, and The Damned Human Race. The now appropriately defunct band Small Girl Boils Water adapted his wretched America into the 21st Century for a rotten song on their lousy self-titled album. He is also a passable visual artist with such dubious credits as the road sign for Little Laurel Preschool and the awful cover illustration for the deplorable Kittens in the Boiler. He lives in barren New Hampshire where he glares at children from his window.

ARYAN KAGANOF drives a 1966 Valiant 200 automatic. He wears Converse All Star sneakers, a Puma jacket and shoots Glock. More information can be found at www.kaganof.com.

JEFF T. KANE is known as the Eric Roberts of the BMX circuit and rides for team Mongoose on a 2004 Mongoose Villain. He occasionally tries his hand at fiction writing. You can buy his book, The Five People You Meet When You Shit Your Pants through www.downsupremacy.blogspot.com

PAUL KAVANAGH was born in England 1971. He is happy. His wife is happy. Together they are happy.

A graduate of the MFA program at Naropa University, **VISHAL KHANNA** writes grants for dermatologists in Winston-Salem, North Carolina. His fiction and nonfiction have been published or is forthcoming in Sun Magazine, Mississippi Review Online, Pindeldyboz and Punk Planet, among other places.

DELPHINE LECOMPTE lives in a drab inhospitable coastal town in northwest Europe. She can shoot an apple off your head with a crossbow. She can hold her breath for two minutes and thirteen seconds. On Sundays she sits on a rooftop and reads James Hadley Chase novels. Her first novel, Kittens in the Boiler, is available through Thieves Jargon Press.

MATT MAXWELL's publishing credits span the gamut, from business journals to mainstream to experimental to gothic horror. Currently, he is a fiction editor with Mad Hatter's Review. His spare time is devoted to reading and writing, and that time is found while recovering from injuries caused by rock climbing and mountain biking.

TOM MEEK is a contributing film critic for the Boston Phoenix and a member of the Boston Society of Film Critics. He can be heard as a regular on WRKO's Taste of Boston Tonight Radio show. His ramblings have appeared in the Fort Worth Star-Telegram, Web del Sol, Film Threat and E! Online. His fiction can be found at The Sink, Thieves Jargon and Word Riot. He lives in Cambridge, practices yoga and rides his bike everywhere. Tom is currently working on a collection of short stories that take place in Boston.

COREY MESLER has been published in numerous magazines and anthologies. His first novel, Talk: a Novel in Dialogue, appeared in 2002 and received kind blurbs from Robert Olen Butler, Frederick Barthelme and John Grisham. His second, We are Billion-Year-Old Carbon, is just out. He has 5 chapbooks due out in 2006. He also claims to have written, "Mmmm-Bop." With his wife he owns Burke's Book Store in Memphis, Tennessee.

SUZANNE NIELSEN has never had an address outside of Minnesota a day in her life. It wasn't until recently, when phone numbers advanced to 10 digits, that she thought of herself as an important contributor to a system held accountable. This is when she became a notary public. She carries her stamp with her at all times just in case of emergencies. Nielsen teaches creative writing at Minneapolis College of Art and Design (MCAD) and Metropolitan State University. Her dissertation explores the question: what makes a good writer a good teacher? It's yet to be officially notarized.

GRANT PERRY's publication credits in print and online include Pindeldyboz, FRiGG, Snow Monkey, Duck & Herring, Eyeshot, Megaera and NOÖ Journal. Excerpts of his never-to-be-completed novel have appeared in The Orphan Leaf Review. Born in Glasgow and raised in Leeds, he now lives in South London.

Over three hundred of **STEPHEN ROGERS'** stories and poems have been selected to appear in more than a hundred publications. His website, www.stephendrogers.com, includes a list of new and upcoming titles as well as other timely information.

A native of Boston, **KEN RYAN** has been published widely, electronically and in print. His first novel, Hiders, was completed in January of 2006. He is currently hard at work on his second novel, a paranormal love story, as well as compiling a collection of short stories. Kenneth currently lives and writes in Winthrop, Massachusetts, snugly nestled on a brief strip of beach between Logan International Airport and the Deer Island Sewage Treatment Plant.

JOE SHOOMAN lives in the UK and one of these days is going to be found out.

PAUL SILVERMAN has worked as a newspaper reporter, sandwich man, olive packer and advertising creative director. One of his commercials won a Silver Lion at Cannes. His stories have appeared in The South Dakota Review, The North Atlantic Review, Thieves Jargon, Word Riot, In Posse Review, The Pedestal Magazine, The Timber Creek Review, The Front Range Review, The Jabberwock Review, Amarillo Bay, The Adirondack Review, The Paumanok Review, The Summerset Review, and others. Byline Magazine and The Worcester Review have nominated his stories to the Pushcart Committee. VerbSap nominated a story for the Million Writers Award. New work was recently accepted by Oyster Boy Review, Tampa Review, Smokelong Quarterly and Jewish Currents.

WILLIE SMITH is deeply ashamed of being human. His work celebrates this horror. His novella SUBMACHINEGUN CONSCIOUSNESS can be read at http://semantikon.com. Novel OEDIPUS CADET available from Black Heron Press. Chapbook GO AHEAD SPIT ON ME too hard to find anyway. He recommends Spider Fuck archived at http://corpse.org. Also salivates a regular online column at 99 BURNING. He intends to stop writing shortly after he is dead, which should be quite soon, as he is fifty-six years of age, unemployed and afflicted with the usual nasty habits.